"Flattery just makes me suspicious, Aden."

Aden pulled her into his arms, startling her. "Why suspicious, Anthea?"

"I—please let go of me, Aden." Anthea's awareness of him was acute. She still didn't trust him wholly and—and she didn't trust herself, either.

Aden suddenly threw back his head and laughed. "Poor Anthea! Anything but being kissed. One of these days my patience and your defenses will run out, and then where will you be?" He pulled her toward him and brought his mouth close to hers. "No, don't look away, I'll answer for you. You'll be in my arms. You'll be in my bed!"

"Aden..."

"You can relax, Anthea," he said, releasing her. "I'm far too proud to seduce you into something you don't want. Something you don't want with your mind, that is."

Claudia Jameson lives in Berkshire, England, with her husband and family. She is an extremely popular author in both the Harlequin Presents and Harlequin Romance series. And no wonder! Her lively dialogue and ingenious plots—with the occasional dash of suspense—make her a favorite with romance readers everywhere.

Books by Claudia Jameson

HARLEQUIN ROMANCE

2578—NEVER SAY NEVER
2594—YOURS...FAITHFULLY
2691—A TIME TO GROW
2842—IMMUNE TO LOVE
2857—A MAN OF CONTRASTS

HARLEQUIN PRESENTS

777—THE FRENCHMAN'S KISS
817—THE SCORPIO MAN
867—ROSES, ALWAYS ROSES
891—THE MAN IN ROOM 12
922—ONE DREAM ONLY
945—ADAM'S LAW
969—TO SPEAK OF LOVE

An Engagement Is Announced

Claudia Jameson

Harlequin Books

TORONTO • NEW YORK • LONDON
AMSTERDAM • PARIS • SYDNEY • HAMBURG
STOCKHOLM • ATHENS • TOKYO • MILAN

Original hardcover edition published in 1987
by Mills & Boon Limited

ISBN 0-373-02878-4

Harlequin Romance first edition December 1987
Second printing November 1987

CHAPTER ONE

'GOOD MORNING, Gail! Glorious, isn't it? How's that for a clear blue sky?' Anthea Norman was frying some bacon, her mouth watering in anticipation. She always ate a hearty breakfast.

'It probably means it's freezing out there.' Her flatmate grunted, and sank on to a chair at the kitchen table. First thing on waking, Gail looked every day of her twenty-seven years. She didn't look after herself properly, that was the trouble, she never ate breakfast, was almost constantly on a diet and if she wasn't working, she was playing. She was hardly ever at rest. 'What are you so happy about?'

'And why are you so glum?' Anthea countered. 'It's your day off, cheer up!'

'Day off? And what am I obliged to do with it? Christmas shopping, that's what!'

Anthea frowned. She had known Gail Brennan for more than five years, had lived with her for the past six months and was used to the grumpiness which always lasted for about an hour after she'd woken up. Happily it didn't last. Once her brain woke up, as she put it, Gail reverted to the bustling, cheerful personality Anthea knew and loved. She was moodier than usual today though, something was wrong. Now was not the time to probe; that had to wait for a more appropriate moment.

Dropping two eggs into the frying pan, Anthea replied laughingly, 'There's no need to panic, it's only the end of

5

November, you've got bags of time.'

Anthea had two weeks off, the second and third weeks of December. Unlike Gail, she would be on duty over Christmas. On the other hand, unlike Gail she was going to spend two weeks in the sun! She was looking forward to that more than she'd looked forward to anything in years, she needed the break. Her work as a physiotherapist was every bit as demanding as Gail's as a nurse, except that the hours were different. Anthea never worked at night and rarely in the evening—unless there was an emergency and she was on call. Gail had night shifts to contend with, not that she ever complained about it. They both loved their work, were both devoted to it. That was the main thing they had in common. They understood and respected each other's dedication, which was probably why they got on so well. They had little else in common yet their friendship was very firm, they'd hit it off together since the moment they'd first met. Gail had cried on her shoulder in those early days and, unexpectedly, shockingly, Anthea had had reason to cry on hers not long after.

That had been in London, at King's College Hospital. Anthea had been a student at the time and Gail, who was three years older, had been working in orthopaedics. She had left Ireland, her family, friends, her job and the husband she'd been briefly married to and had come to London to begin a new life. In time she had told Anthea all there was to know about her. In time her divorce had come through and, in time, her attitude towards men, understandably bitter, had changed. These days she was never without a boyfriend, never without a date when she wanted one.

Anthea's home was in the Midlands, not that she

thought in those terms any longer. Her *family* was in the Midlands. Home, now, was here in Guildford, Surrey. She too had begun a new life the day she'd left Bromsgrove to start her training as a physiotherapist. Her ideas of moving back to the Midlands had long since been abandoned. Life was just as she wanted it to be at long last, it was orderly and satisfactory, more than satisfactory. It was under her control . . . or so she liked to think. Actually, nobody knew better than she how helpless, how powerless one was if Fate decided to step in. The death of her fiancé had taught her that lesson. A hard lesson, a painful one. But Tony's death had been almost five years ago, she was over it now. Over it and yet . . . wary. She was wary of involvement; never again did she want to go through the heartbreak of loving and losing. At twenty-four she was a very different person from the one she had been when she'd left home.

She and Gail had been a comfort to each other when they'd met, they still were, and it bothered her to see Gail looking so tired. They hardly ever went out together socially, they seemed to be as different as chalk and cheese, but they each knew the other was *there*. Flat-mate, friend, confidante. Gail had been the first to move to Guildford, having left King's College Hospital to work at St Bartholomew's before taking the post at the general hospital here. That had been ten months ago. Anthea had followed four months later, never having lost contact with Gail over the years. They lived separately together now, pursuing their own life-styles, sharing expenses, which made things easier. It was an ideal arrangement.

Life was good, which was precisely why Anthea was in a particularly happy mood this morning. She had been taking stock and found she had no complaints at all.

'It's all right for you,' Gail said again. 'You're going to a party tonight and in a couple of weeks you'll take off for the Canary Islands. Mind you,' she added, sipping at a cup of tea, 'I don't envy you either of those things. Well, the sunshine, perhaps, but not the company.'

Anthea was taken aback. Her mouth opened and closed, the protest dying in her throat. Gail really was in an odd mood today! It was she who'd talked Anthea into accepting the invitation to holiday in the Canary Islands. 'Tenerife?' she'd said. 'You've been invited to spend two weeks in a private villa in Tenerife and you're asking me whether you should accept? Are you nuts? Of course you should accept! You'd be mad not to!'

And now this. Quietly, she asked Gail what was wrong. The answer was short and a little sharp. 'Nothing.'

'All right, I'll ask you again later—when your brain's woken up.' Anthea spoke patiently, smiling. She did not expect to be snapped at again, harshly this time.

'What is it with you, Anthea? How do you manage to stay constantly on an even keel? It isn't normal. You never get ruffled, you smile your angelic smile at the drop of a hat and you have an attitude towards life like that of Pollyanna.'

There was no chance to answer. Gail went on, her soft, southern Irish brogue more pronounced—as it always was when she was wound-up about something. 'Worse, you look as fresh as a daisy at all hours of the day, you eat like a gannet and never put on an ounce and you haven't the faintest idea how attractive you are. Pale blonde locks, natural at that, big blue eyes, slender figure—and where does it get you? Who gets to enjoy it all? Not you, that's for sure!'

This time Anthea's mouth fell open. Gail wasn't making much sense. What was this? 'Gail——'

'Look at you, at your life. Where is it heading?'

'My life? What's wrong with it?'

'Nothing. Everything. Oh, it's too—too *bland*!' Gail's teacup hit the saucer with a smack. She was shaking her head in disgust, her unruly hair shifting around her face. The roots needed doing again.

'Bland?'

'Bland. There are no highs, no lows. It worries me.'

Anthea pushed her chair away from the table slightly, crossed one long, slender leg over the other and folded her arms. 'OK, that's enough of this nonsense. What's up? Why am I in the firing line?'

'See what I mean?' Gail rummaged in the pockets of her housecoat and pulled out a packet of cigarettes. 'Even when I insult you, you don't react.'

'You're not insulting me, don't be daft. Somebody or something has upset you. Last night. Now then, who were you with last night ... aha! Our newest registrar, was it not? Gordon Langley! So what happened? You discovered he's not as charming as he appears, right?'

It was Gail's turn to be taken aback. She let out a long sigh, lit her cigarette and averted her eyes. 'Sorry,' she said at length, her voice dull. 'I'm sorry, Anthea. Don't know what's got into me today.'

'You've only just got up.'

'I'm not usually this bad.'

'True. So?'

'So Gordon fancies you. You, not me.'

It wasn't exactly news to Anthea, she'd known it from her first encounter with the doctor. He'd started work at the hospital just five weeks earlier and had asked her out twice. She'd refused, politely, nicely, but without explanation. Why should she explain? The man fancied himself. How popular he would prove with the male staff had yet to be seen—but almost all the females were already under his spell. Gail, by the look of it, especially.

'The evening was a wash-out,' she complained. 'When he came to collect me, he asked after you. Wanted to know if you were out on a date. I said I didn't know where you were. I assume you were with your old lady, Sybil?'

Anthea shook her head. 'I was at that lecture I mentioned to you. Sybil had asked me to dinner, actually, she's been looking forward to my meeting her nephew. He was driving down from London yesterday to spend the weekend with her. She's delighted about that, she doesn't see him as often as she'd like to. Still, I'll be meeting him tonight so that'll make her happy. Anyhow, never mind that, what about Gordon?'

Gail shrugged. 'Nothing. Oh, he was charm personified, but we just didn't click. When we were half-way through our meal I realised why he'd asked me out. He wanted to know about you. You've got him intrigued. I came to the conclusion he'd asked me out just to get an insight about you!'

Anthea groaned inwardly. She didn't question Gail's conclusion. She was shrewd, a good judge of character generally, and she had more experience when it came to men, far more. Anthea looked at her watch. She had to go. There was a busy day ahead of her, she was working in out-patients at the hospital this morning, doing rounds on the wards after lunch, and then she had some private patients to see. After that it would be a dash home, a quick change and off to Sybil's birthday party. She had been asked to go early. It was a good job it was Friday, she could lie in in the morning. Well, within reason. She got to her feet. 'I'm off.'

'Hey—is that all you've got to say?'

'About what?'

'About Gordon, of course. You, me, him.'

Anthea smiled, shrugging. 'If he is interested in me—intrigued, to use your word—he's wasting his time. He is absolutely one hundred per cent not my type——'

'If I had a pound for the number of times I've heard you say that about a man! You haven't got a "type", let's face it.'

'And if he really was using you to get information about me, it turns me off even more. I'm sorry, Gail, but it's hardly my fault. As for you, you'll get over it quickly enough. You spend half your time complaining about how you look, yet you can pull any man you set your sights on.' It was true, Gail was on the plump side in spite of her diets, her blonde hair was bleached and unruly, her dress-sense nothing to write home about. Yet somehow she managed to be very attractive; her personality was her best asset. That and her often impish sense of humour.

'Hardly! I happen to fancy Gordon Langley.'

'I can see right through you. Gordon's become a challenge, plain and simple. Got to go, love, I'll be late.'

Gail was exasperated. 'You're never late, you're always at work half an hour before you need to be. Hang on a jiff, I want to apologise——'

'There's no need for that!'

'There is, Anthea. Look, I—I'm sorry, I have a bad case of sour grapes, I shouldn't have attacked you. Kindly stop being so patient with me because there's something I do want to say, something I've been thinking for a while. It has nothing to do with Gordon and it's going to annoy you good and proper.'

'To be sure.'

'*Anthea*, will you please——'

'All right, all right, what is it?' Anthea sat down again. It was true, she was in no danger of being late for work. Whatever was bothering Gail would be better brought out into the open.

'It is simply this,' Gail said quietly, holding up both hands as if to defend herself. 'Since you came to Guildford, you've changed. Again. This time, well, I'm not saying it's for the worse but you *are* starting to worry me. There's as much social life here as there was available in London, there are as many opportunities, I told you that before you moved here.'

Anthea listened, having no idea where this was leading. Opportunities for what? 'You've been here six months,' Gail went on, 'and you've changed, as I say. You're becoming . . . I don't know how to decribe it. You've turned in on yourself.'

'What?'

'You're getting to be antisocial. You hardly go out these days. Except to see Sybil.'

'I'm very fond of Sybil——'

'I know, I know. But she's an old lady of seventy-odd and I can't imagine what you find to talk to her about. As for going on holiday with her——'

'Gail, what *is* the matter with you? It was you who said I should!'

'I know. Maybe it was bad advice. I think you might be bored out of your mind.'

'This is ridiculous. Firstly I'm by no means antisocial and secondly, if I'm not bored here, I'm not going to be bored on a pretty island, basking in the sun!'

'Maybe, but it isn't just that. It's Sybil herself, she seems to be having a peculiar influence on you.'

'Gail, I haven't the faintest idea what you're talking about. Please get to the point.'

'Right. You're becoming a drag.'

Anthea stared at her. 'I beg your pardon?'

'You heard. I burn the candle at both ends, so to speak, and you don't. Fine. But you're beginning to affect me, and that's not fine. You're getting more and more pernickety about housework, you've started to complain if I don't tidy up meticulously after myself, you keep turning the radio down. To cap it all, last week when I was in the living-room with Paul Patterson you walked through to the kitchen and made some snide remark about the time.'

Snide? Snide! It had been three in the morning, the hi-fi was on and it had woken her. She'd gone in to the kitchen to get some milk, that was all. She pointed this out now.

'I didn't finish my shift till ten,' Gail reminded her. 'The fact that it was three in the morning was irrelevant. You walked in on me and Paul and you behaved more like my granny than my flat-mate. Do you see what I mean? It has to stop, Anthea.'

She didn't know what to say. Was it true? Was she getting pernickety, antisocial? Had her thinking changed? If so, how much? That she was very different from her eighteen-year-old self, she knew, but how much had she changed during the last six months? 'I've got to go,' she said quietly. 'I—we'll finish this conversation some other time.'

Conversation? It was the closest she had ever come to arguing with Gail. Had she not been taking stock of her life that very morning, it might have developed into a row. There again it might not. Anthea wasn't the type to get involved in rows. Which was precisely the point: she *was* constantly on an even keel. She used to flare up easily, to be quite temperamental, easily hurt, easily upset. These days she wasn't, she had thought that a good thing, had thought it a positive kind of growth. Wasn't it?

Gail had shaken her, had shaken her confidence and her self-image. By lunch time she found herself resenting her friend, by mid-afternoon she found herself giving her the benefit of the doubt. Maybe she was getting to be a bit stuffy, maybe she should go out more, have some fun . . .

It was hardly Sybil's fault, though! If she were different these days, it was hardly attributable to her. Throughout the latter part of the day bits of conversations with Sybil kept popping into Anthea's head. She had known Sybil for three months, from the time she had suffered a mild stroke. Sybil hadn't been hospitalised for long, Anthea had continued to treat her during home visits after her discharge and they'd become friendly. They had spent hours talking together, during physiotherapy sessions and, as time passed, over tea or dinner. No, Sybil hadn't had a peculiar influence on her. How could Gail think that, especially when she hadn't even met Sybil? Sybil Manly-Smythe was a very sweet and very likeable old lady, lady being the operative word.

Born in India when the British ruled there, her

upbringing had been fascinating. To Anthea, anyhow. Maybe Gail would never understand it but she loved listening to Sybil's stories about her life there so many decades ago. From the age of thirty, having moved back to England ten years earlier, Sybil had worked for the Foreign Office until her retirement. There was a lot more to her than one would guess at first meeting; she was sharp-witted, clever and courageous.

It had been in the hospital that Anthea had been regaled with the virtues of Russell Manly-Smythe, Sybil's favourite nephew.

'Russ visited again last night, that's my nephew, you know.'

'Yes, I remember your saying——'

'Such a fine young man! Well, I suppose he's not *so* young any more. He's thirty-six. And a confirmed bachelor, more's the pity. Such a waste . . . Do you know, he's been to see me almost every evening? It's so sweet of him because he's extremely busy. Did I mention he's a barrister? He's a QC. Queen's Counsel at thirty-six, he's doing very well, don't you think?'

Anthea had never set eyes on the man but she knew a lot about him. He was Sybil's pride and joy. So clever, so successful, according to Sybil. And handsome, according to Sybil. And kind and generous and sensitive—according to Sybil!

It was 'Russ this, Russ that'. The villa in Tenerife belonged to him—which was the reason for Anthea's hesitation when Sybil had asked her to take a holiday with her there. There had been no other reason for hesitating.

Russ wanted his aunt to take a long holiday, to recuperate thoroughly after her illness. Three months, he said, she should get away from the cold English winter for at least three months.

'Which is quite ridiculous,' Sybil had explained to Anthea, smiling and shaking her head at the same time. 'Of course he means well. But three months? I should be so bored! I don't speak any Spanish. I couldn't even have a conversation with the maid! No, I had to put my foot down with Russ. I agreed to go for one month, which I'm sure will be quite nice. It's in . . . I can't recall the name of the area. Oh, well! Anyway, he assures me it's very pleasant, very pleasant indeed. And there's a swimming pool—his own, of course. Quite a large one if the photographs are anything to go by. Russ spends as much time as he can there. Even so, he obviously can't take three months off work, he said the most he can manage is a couple of weeks. So what do you say, Anthea? Won't you come? Do say yes!'

'I'd love to but . . .'

'But what, dear?'

'Well, it's very kind of you to ask me——'

'It was Russell's suggestion, actually. Oh, dear me! That doesn't sound too good, does it? What I mean is, it was his suggestion and I thought it brilliant.'

Anthea had still been dubious. Virtually anything Russ suggested would sound brilliant to his aunt. Still, it was so very tempting . . .

'Are you thinking about your own family, Anthea? Is that why you hesitate? Shall they miss you? Of course they'll miss you. You want to spend your holidays with them.'

'No, it isn't that.' Her own family? They all lived in Bromsgrove, her parents, aunts, uncles and cousins, her three sisters with their respective husbands and children.

In truth, Anthea was something of the black sheep these days, she had been since she'd left the Midlands to study in London. She could have trained nearer home but she had chosen not to. Somehow her family had never quite forgiven her for that—for the way she'd changed over the years.

'Then what is it?' Sybil had persisted. 'Ah! Is it money? *I* shall buy your air ticket, we'll regard it as a Christmas present.'

'No! Absolutely not. I won't even consider it. Besides, that isn't the problem. It's just—well, I—I haven't even met Russ.' How could she live with a total stranger for two weeks? A stranger she didn't even like the sound of, in all honesty!

'Which is something we must rectify as soon as possible. Such a pity you weren't in when I phoned you last week, when he dropped in unexpectedly. I had hoped you'd get to meet him then.'

The conversation had gone on, though it was several minutes before Anthea realised that the precious Russell wasn't going to be in Tenerife at the same time as she. He was going to fly out on the day after she came home. His two-week holiday would stretch either side of Christmas. Nevertheless she'd still hesitated, asking Sybil to give her a little time to think it over. What she'd really wanted was to ask Gail's opinion, and she had been very enthusiastic—until this morning.

Gail wasn't in when Anthea got home that night. Anthea was sorry about that; the unfinished conversation of the morning was still bothering her. The air had to be cleared, certain points had to be dealt with. Heaven knew she had given it enough thought; she'd decided it had been wrong of her to complain about the noise from the hi-fi last week. Compromise was called for when you lived with someone.

As for the rest of it—Gail was wrong. Just because Anthea didn't date a string of men simultaneously, it didn't mean she was a drag. Nor had she turned 'in' on herself, whatever that meant. She had simply acquired peace, a routine and way of life which suited her. It was an achievement that had taken some years. After Tony's sudden death there had been so much confusion, so many adjustments to make. Her entire future had changed drastically, her aims and ambitions likewise.

She couldn't soak for long in the bath before dressing for the party that evening, which was something else she was sorry about. She made up her face as sparingly as she did each morning and climbed into a simple jersey dress in royal blue. It did things for her eyes—not that she was out to impress anyone. Most of the guests at Sybil's seventy-third birthday party would be strangers to her. A wry smile touched her lips. By now she could stop thinking of Russ as such, since she'd heard so much about the man, she felt she knew him already.

Sybil clearly adored the man, although, to give her her due, she did resist his influence, his dictates, to some extent. Hers was a fiercely independent spirit; she lived alone and that's how she liked it. 'I've lived alone since I came here from India. That was fifty-two years ago and I'm not about to change things now. In fact I think it's silly my having a housekeeper, albeit a part-timer. But Russ insisted I have some help. If he had his way, I'd be stuck with a living-in housekeeper. No privacy at all! . . . Of course Louise and Rodney would love me to go and live with them but the same applies. They mention it every time they write.'

Louise and Rodney, now which ones were they? Oh, yes, the ones who lived in Hong Kong—but whose progeny were they? Anthea hadn't been able to remember at the time. There was more than Russ to Sybil's family, many more! She had nephews and nieces dotted all over the globe. She had been the youngest of six children, all of whom were now dead, all of whom had married, except herself.

'Louise? I've forgotten whose child she is, Sybil.'

'Not Louise, dear. Rodney. Louise was a Rowbottom before she married Rodney. Rodney is Montgomery's son, Montgomery being my youngest brother. It does get confusing, doesn't it?'

'Frankly, yes! Now I know how other people feel when I talk about my family—there are so many of them!'

'You have three sisters, haven't you? And you're the baby, like me.' There had been a chuckle at that. 'Do tell me more about them, Anthea. And what about your parents . . .?'

Anthea drove to Sybil's house thinking about all this, about Sybil's relatives and her own, about the past and the present. By the time she pulled on to the drive a steady drizzle was falling. Three other cars were parked on the drive, one of them a dark Rolls Royce. Three guesses who that belonged to! Sybil didn't own a car— and it certainly wasn't the housekeeper's.

Shivering, she pulled her wrap around her shoulders and dashed for the front door, her thoughts switching to sunshine and swimming and sand. She would enjoy herself in Tenerife with Sybil. It made no difference to Anthea that they were fifty years apart in age and there was no question of being bored!

Glancing down at the beautifully wrapped gift in her

hands, she rang the door bell.

It wasn't Sybil who answered. Nor was it a stranger. The light from the hall combined with the outside light and gave Anthea clear sight of the man who was holding the door open. Her eyes widened in disbelief, the smile fading rapidly from her lips. Him? Him! What was *he* doing here? Here, at Sybil's? It had been a long time since Anthea had last seen him, four years and ten months precisely. Oh, yes, she remembered exactly! How could she forget?

He recognised her, too. There was no smile on his face, not exactly, it was more of a smirk than a smile, and there was something in his eyes which told her he'd known her at once. And so he should, the swine. He'd reduced her to tears on more than one occasion!

CHAPTER TWO

ANTHEA was still staring, unable to believe their paths had crossed again. All right, Guildford wasn't far from London but . . . but *why* was he here, at Sybil's birthday party?

Sybil appeared at the door, poking her head round the man's frame to peer outside. It wasn't the easiest thing to do because he was very big, very broad, his body almost filling the doorway. 'What is it?' she asked. 'Who—it's you, Anthea!' She shot a look of puzzlement at the man. 'What on earth are you thinking about? Don't keep Anthea standing on the doorstep, she'll freeze! Come in, dear, come in out of the cold.'

Anthea was ushered inside, unable to find her voice. The man stepped aside to let her pass and the three of them stood in the hall. She couldn't take her eyes off him.

'Give me your wrap,' Sybil was saying. 'I'll put it in the cloakroom, but let me introduce you two first.' Her voice softened, she was beaming suddenly. 'I've been longing for you to meet. Anthea,' she went on, quite formal now, 'I'd like you to meet my nephew, Russ. Russ, this is Anthea Norman. Now then! Isn't she every bit as pretty as I've told you she is?'

He said nothing for the moment, he merely looked at Anthea, fixing her with clear green eyes full of amusement. She remembered those eyes. Among other things. She remembered them well, they'd unnerved her years ago as they were unnerving her now. She couldn't

21

find her voice, for the life of her she couldn't even put a smile on her face, there was too much resentment in her, too much confusion. Russ? *This* was Sybil's nephew? Well, he hadn't been called Russ when she'd known him! He'd had a very unusual name, she couldn't recall what it was but it wasn't Russell Manly-Smythe! Bewildered, she turned to Sybil.

He got in first, however. He spoke in a drawl, a voice drenched with irony, his eyes positively dancing with laughter now. 'No, Sybil,' he said, 'she's even prettier than your description.' It was only then that he held out his hand.

Automatically, Anthea took it. Her hand was clasped briefly in a bone-crunching grip before she pulled away, before she realised she simply must tell Sybil the truth.

But, again, he got in first. 'How very nice to see you again, Miss Norman.' One eyebrow quirked as he saw the look of astonishment on his aunt's face. 'That's right, darling. Quite a surprise, isn't it? Miss Norman and I have met before.'

'Good heavens! Well, I never! But how, when? Where——'

'Four years ago. Almost five. Let me see . . .' He turned back to Anthea. 'If I remember correctly, and I do because I have an excellent memory, it's four years and ten months.'

'You remember correctly,' she managed. Having found her voice, she went on. 'Your nephew was a patient in King's College Hospital and——'

'And Miss Norman was a student at the time. She practised on me,' he added, with a significance only Anthea could interpret. She opened her mouth to protest but he went on. 'That car crash, Sybil, remember? When that idiot dolly-bird smashed into me?'

'Of course I remember! But—well, fancy! I hadn't realised Anthea did her training at that hospital. You never mentioned it, dear.'

With infuriating joviality her nephew suggested he take Anthea through to the living-room. 'Why don't I give your guest a drink while you do something with that wrap? I'm sure Miss Norman and I can find lots to talk about . . .'

Sybil, looking extremely pleased about the whole thing, disappeared along the hall with Anthea's wrap. As soon as her back was turned Anthea pulled her arm from the man's grasp. She wasn't going anywhere just yet. 'Just a moment, Mr . . . whoever you are. You weren't called Manly-Smythe five years ago.'

He was grinning now, obviously enjoying her discomfiture, her shock at seeing him again. 'That's true.'

'But . . . Don't *do* that!' He'd put his hand on her arm again. She glared at him, her head tilted so she could look directly in to his eyes. He towered over her by some six inches in spite of her high-heeled boots. He had changed only minimally, his jet black hair was tinged with silver at the temples now. It was thick and straight, he still wore it brushed straight back from his face. It was a strong face, a good indication of his character what with that deep cleft in the chin, a square, unyielding jaw. Nothing was changed except, somehow, it was more handsome now than it had been—which impressed her not in the least. 'There are one or two things we must clear up.'

'You do realise you're still clutching Sybil's present? I presume that's for her.'

'What? Oh! Yes, I—I'll give it to her later. Now kindly tell me something. You knew, didn't you? You knew before I got here that I was coming. I mean, what I mean is——' she broke of, irritated. He was still laughing at her, she could see it in his eyes. She drew a deep breath in an effort to compose herself. 'Since Sybil's told me a lot about you, I assume she's told you a lot about me. You must have recognised my name, my physical description. Why didn't you tell her you knew me?'

He considered for a moment, and when he answered she didn't believe him. 'Because I couldn't be sure, could I? There must be thousands of blondes by the name of Anthea in this world. Of course they're not all beautiful, they're not all physiotherapists . . .'

'And they don't all have Norman as a surname. You knew it was me, you have an excellent memory, you said so yourself.'

'Ah! But you were wearing an engagement ring when those pretty little hands of yours were ministering to me. It was a scrap of emerald, right?' he added, glancing at her left hand. 'And now it's gone—with nothing to replace it.'

Anthea looked down at the carpet, struggling to control herself. How was she going to get through this evening? This bear of a man was needling her now as he'd needled her in the past. He was right about the ring. She still had it, that 'scrap' of emerald, as he disparagingly put it. 'There is nothing in this world,' she said slowly, looking directly in to his eyes, 'that could replace that ring.'

He inclined his head. 'How very dramatic you are! I'm curious. What happened?'

Anthea turned away.

'Why so resentful, Angel Face?'

She stopped in her tracks. Angel Face! That's what

he'd called her that first day, *her* first day, one she would never forget.

She had been nineteen at the time, into her second year of training and about to handle a real, live patient for the first time. God, she'd been nervous! A real live patient—and it had been her misfortune to be introduced to this man. Had he behaved like a normal human being, there would have been no problem. His case had been perfectly straightforward, all he'd needed as far as physiotherapy was concerned was, mainly, manipulation of the elbow joint. But no, he'd been like a bear with a sore head, unutterably rude and completely lacking in tolerance.

She could hear his voice now, could recall exactly the words he'd used. 'A student?' he'd said to her supervisor. 'You're asking me to let this little girl have a go at me? How old are you, Angel Face?' he'd demanded, turning to the stricken Anthea. 'Never mind, just clear out and send in your mother instead.' Then, shaking his head at the older woman, 'Dammit all, isn't it bad enough that I have to lie in this bed for several days? Are you seriously asking me to be some kind of guinea-pig? This *child* surely hasn't the strength to give someone a massage, let alone anything else!'

'That's precisely what she's going to do, among other things.' Mrs Eversley had stood no nonsense. She'd handled the man beautifully, with patience and tact. 'I'm sure the entire hospital is aware of your frustrations,' she said smoothly. 'You can't wait to get back to work and your normal routine. Well, Mr Russell, the sooner we——'

Russell. *Mister* Russell. The name had come back to Anthea in a flash. 'Mr Russell,' she said to him now. 'Aden. You were *Aden Russell* five years ago.'

'I still am,' he said. 'Come on, we can't stand in the hall all evening.'

'But——'

'My dear Miss Norman, I shall explain later all you wish to know and, unless you're as scatty now as you were when we first met, you'll find it very simple to understand.'

Unfortunately she had no choice but to follow him into the living-room. He strode away—but she managed a retort before they joined the other guests. 'Scatty! You've got a nerve! It's quite obvious that time has done nothing for your manners. You're as obnoxious——' There wasn't time for more. They were face to face with the vicar, a dear friend of Sybil's and one of the few people present who Anthea had met before.

It was a strange evening, strange and very disturbing. It was difficult not to keep looking at Aden Russell even when she was talking to other people. That was the type of party it was, with people sitting and standing around in groups, swapping around now and then when introductions were made. There was no music, not that she had expected it, and the supper was buffet-style.

'Russ wanted to bring caterers in,' Sybil said at one point, though not directly to Anthea, who was merely standing within earshot, involved in small-talk with a Sir Michael and Lady Florence Morrisey. 'But I said no, absolutely ridiculous. I said I'm not having that sort of party, darling, there'll be no more than twenty people at the most and I shall expect them all to have left by ten-thirty.'

'Michael, Florence, let me give you a refill.' The hair at the back of Anthea's neck prickled at the sound of Aden's voice behind her. 'And what about you, Miss

Norman? You've hardly touched your drink, would you prefer something else?'

'No thank you,' she said crisply. 'I'm driving.' What was it about this man? How could he speak with such a well modulated voice, with such apparent charm, at the moment, and manage at the same time to convey nothing but sarcasm? To her at least. Nobody else seemed to notice it. Lady Florence was almost batting her eyelashes at him.

'Yes, please, Aden. It's very sweet of you to look after Sybil's guests yourself.'

'I had no choice,' he replied, raising his voice. 'My aunt is so stubborn, as we're all well aware; she refused point blank to let me bring caterers in.'

Sybil rose to it at once. There was a sudden shifting among the gatherings, like musical chairs without the music and chairs. 'What was that, Russell?'

'I said you're stubborn, Sybil. I think everyone heard me—including you.'

'Impudent!'

Anthea had to look away. She couldn't help it, she found it disturbing that Sybil, whom she respected very much, could think so highly, could be so obviously fond, of a man who was blatantly arrogant. Well, he was family, she supposed . . .

As it turned out, that particular matter was cleared up a few minutes later—when Aden lured Anthea away from the group.

'Come and give me a hand,' he said, his fingers closing so tightly around her arm, it was all she could do not to wince. 'By the way, Florence, did you know Miss Norman and I are old friends?'

'Really?'

'Oh, yes!' He smiled, a smile so full and charming Lady Florence flushed a little. Anthea was disgusted. 'In fact, any moment now she'll invite me to call her Anthea, you'll see!'

She waited until they were out of the room before trying to wrench free of him. 'Stop doing that. You're hurting me!'

'What a shame.' He laughed outrageously, his hand tightening so hard that she yelped. 'So the score's even. You hurt me once, remember?'

She hadn't planned to hurt him, though when she did it was quite deliberate. He'd been sarcastic every time she'd seen him, chipping at her, putting her down, muttering while she was treating him so only she could hear.

'You don't look old enough to have left school.' 'I'd have thought you more suited to modelling than ministering.' And once, when she was massaging his back, 'Is that the best you can do? I have to say, my girlfriend does it better and she only works on instinct.'

He'd turned to look at her, caught her blushing. 'What's the matter? Does that embarrass you? It won't do to be easily embarrassed in this job. Was it my remark or is it my near nudity?'

If she were to encounter someone like that these days it wouldn't worry her in the least, she would give as good as she got. But she'd been only nineteen when she'd had to cope with Aden Russell, green as far as people and the world were concerned, nineteen and nervous, lacking in confidence and very easily upset. Not that she had let him know it. She had never answered him back, rather she'd blushed and fumed inwardly, giving vent to her frustrations later, complaining about him to fellow students or to her fiancé if she saw him. On two occasions she had been so angry, she'd burst into tears after treating Aden Russell.

How silly she'd been! Revenge had been sweet, though, except that her patient had known full well she'd hurt him on purpose. 'I see,' he'd said, 'you're trying to break my arm now, mm?'

The memory gave her a certain pleasure now, as he steered her in to the kitchen, where the drinks were. 'I remember it well,' he was saying. 'You were a funny little creature, one would never have suspected you had sadistic tendencies.'

'I was nervous, shy and inexperienced. And you were a pig.'

Only then did he let go of her. 'Oh, come, come now. I teased you, that's all.'

'Teased? *Teased!* Is that what you call it? You—oh, never mind! Since you've known all along that it was I treating your aunt, how come you didn't warn her off? After all, you have a vision of me as totally incompetent.'

'What nonsense. You must have qualified or you wouldn't be where you are now.'

She'd qualified all right, with distinction. 'I became a Member of the Chartered Society of Physiotherapists when I was twenty-one, for your information. I am extremely good at what I do.'

'So Sybil tells me. She speaks *very* highly of you.' He didn't look up from what he was doing, pouring drinks. 'Still touchy, aren't you? Do you still blush as furiously as you used to?' He turned, his manner autocratic now. 'Make yourself useful. Grab that tray over there and take these.'

She ignored him. 'Mr Russell, I'd like to point out——'

'Ah, yes, about that. Everyone calls me Aden, as you may or may not have observed, except members of my family. That's because my father, whose name was also Aden, had the surname of Russell. Are you with me so far, Angel Face? My father and I had the same names. He's dead now, of course, but you can imagine the confusion years ago, when the family spoke to me and he answered, or vice versa. So they took to calling me Russ to avoid confusion. The name stuck. Force of habit. You're looking blank, Anthea my old friend, has it been too much for you to take in?'

'I'll ignore that. I'd thought you were Sybil's brother's son.'

'Wrong. My mother was Melissa, her sister. She was one year older than Sybil and she died two years ago.'

'She must have had you quite late in life.'

'She did, she was thirty-eight at the time and, in case you're wondering, I was her one and only.' He picked up the tray and put several glasses on it. 'Now supposing you tell me something,' he added, thrusting the tray at her. 'What happened to your engagement?'

She took the tray, she had no choice. But she didn't have to answer his questions. 'That's none of your business.'

He smiled, put both hands on her cheeks and tutted. 'How touchy you are!'

And he was clever. He had her cornered, holding the tray, unable to slap his hands away. His handsome face was too close to hers, his hands warm against her cheeks. It bothered her enormously. That and his attitude. She snapped at him, thinking that if it weren't for Sybil, she'd walk away from this party right now. As it was, she couldn't, she'd only been here an hour. 'Go to hell, Mr

Russell! Just leave me alone, will you?'

But he wasn't looking at her now. He was looking over her shoulder. 'Ah, Vicar . . .'

Anthea spun round, the drinks on the tray slopping around in their glasses. It really was the vicar—looking bemused. 'Sorry to interrupt,' he said. 'I believe that's your Metro on the drive, Anthea?'

She hardly knew where to look. 'Yes, I—yes.'

'Then perhaps you'd be kind enough to move it, please? You're blocking my car and I must be off now.'

'Oh! Of course, I—er——' She glanced at Aden, pushed the tray towards him. 'Will you take this?' Dammit, he was laughing at her again, his green eyes were sparkling with it.

'I'll do better than that. I'll move your car for you. It's pouring out there.'

'Don't bother,' she said sweetly, for the benefit of the vicar, 'I won't melt. You'd better take these drinks to your guests before they die of thirst.'

She was fuming when she got in her car. What rotten luck, having the vicar overhear like that! What must he think? He must at least be wondering why she was being rude to Sybil's nephew. Sybil's nephew—she should have let him move her car, after all. The rain was coming in torrents, the short walk from the house had soaked her. She backed off the drive and on to the road, wishing she could keep on driving and go home.

Thankfully she wasn't bothered by Aden Russell again. He was ensconced in conversation with an elderly, bearded foreigner when Anthea went back to the living-room. Sybil beckoned her, admonishing her for buying an extravagant gift. 'It's really naughty of you, Anthea. But thank you. It's a beautiful shawl.'

'Listen,' Sybil went on, lowering her voice conspiratorially. 'You must stay when everyone else has gone, have a nightcap with me and Russ.'

'Well, actually——'

'No arguments.' Sybil's thin hand fluttered dismissively. 'You must humour me, it's my birthday. Besides, you and Russ are my favourite people, don't you know that? I love having young people around me.'

Anthea smiled. Sybil was such a sweetheart. 'Very well, since it's your birthday and you're laying down the law!' What else could she say? It was very flattering to be regarded as a favourite by this old lady. What she didn't understand was why. It wasn't as if she could entertain Sybil, as she was entertained. Nevertheless, it was obvious Sybil's compliment was sincere.

It was almost midnight when Anthea finally got away. By then she was very much her usual self again, taking her leave because Sybil was tired and it showed. They'd had a pleasant hour, the three of them, in the room Sybil called her 'den', and Aden had behaved impeccably. There had been no jibes, no sarcasm, nothing. Nothing but charm. Not that that fooled her, he was behaving for his aunt's sake. Which made two of them.

'I must go, Sybil.'

'Not yet! You're not working tomorrow, are you?'

'No, I shall be having a lovely lie in. But you're tired.'

There was a chuckle. 'Who says?'

'I do.' Anthea picked up her handbag. She was aware of being scrutinised, of Aden watching the interplay. 'And you can't fool me. No, no, don't get up, I know my way out.'

'I'll see you out,' her nephew said.

'There's really no need . . .' It was wasted breath..He

escorted her to the door just the same.

'Well, goodnight, Aden.' She'd had to address him as such; Sybil had protested when she kept calling him 'Mr Russell'. 'I can't say it's been pleasant,' she went on, 'not altogether. But there we are. As long as Sybil's happy.'

There was no smile, no sarcasm even now they were alone. 'As long as Sybil's happy,' he repeated. 'Quite so. Now when can we meet, you and I? Alone. Do you ever go into London?'

Astonished, Anthea told him she often went into London. 'But why should you want to see me alone?'

There was the slightest hesitation. They were in the porch, standing close, and he reached out, thought better of it and dropped his hand. 'I've just remembered your aversion to being touched. There are several possible answers to your question, Anthea. However, all I want is to talk to you in private.'

'The answer's no.'

'The answer's yes. It's about Sybil.'

'It's still no.' She drew her wrap closely around her shoulders and opened the outer door. 'I can tell you now what you want to know. Your aunt is well. Given her age, she's remarkable. Her recovery from the stroke has been most satisfactory, as you can surely see for yourself. She has full mobility and her balance is as good as it was before she took ill. Goodnight.' And with that she walked off. They would meet again, some time or other, that was inevitable, but she was damned if she'd agree to spend time alone with him. Ever.

CHAPTER THREE

'OF COURSE I don't remember him,' said Gail. 'Should I?
Maybe I wasn't on his ward.' She had been up and
dressed by the time Anthea surfaced at a little after ten.
She had to be at the hospital by noon. 'Anyway, how was
the party? Is there any more tea in the pot?'

'Gail, will you listen to me? You weren't working on
his ward—you were in maternity at the time! But—can't
you remember my moaning about him?'

'Aden Russell? No, can't say I do.' She looked more
closely at Anthea. 'Hey, you're really ruffled, aren't you?
What about him then? Tell me all!'

Anthea did just that. They had an hour before Gail had
to leave for work. 'It was the month before Tony was
killed,' she began. She told her flat-mate everything,
every detail of her experience with Aden when she was a
student, bringing her right up to date with last night's
encounter, in detail. 'Things might have been quite
different if he hadn't been so sarcastic. I mean, *I'm*
different, very, but he isn't. I found him as offensive last
night as I had before. He's rude, arrogant and he's a
clever dick. There's no . . . Gail, why are you laughing
like that?'

Gail was laughing so hard she had to put her cup
down. 'Because I'm delighted. You fancy him, it's as
plain as the nose on your face.'

'*Fancy him?* You must be joking!'

'I'm not joking. With the exception of Tony, I have

34

never heard you talk so long about one man before.'

'That doesn't mean——'

'What's more, you're blushing. This is great!' she added gleefully. 'He's got right under your skin. I can't wait to meet him. The man who can do this to you has to be something special.'

Anthea couldn't believe this. 'There's nothing special about him. Yes, he's good-looking. No one's denying that. But I, unlike you, require more than that in a man.'

'Thanks. Considering the last date you accepted was about eight months ago, you must "require" a hell of a lot!'

'I do. Courtesy and sensitivity for starters.'

'Oh, come off it, Anthea. The man's well bred and well educated, isn't he? You've got the wrong impression, that's all. You should have agreed to see him alone, got to know him better.'

Anthea shoved her chair away from the table and started stacking the breakfast things. 'There's no point in continuing this conversation. Let's talk about us instead, about our conversation yesterday. You were saying that when you and Paul Patterson were—oh, my God!'

'What is it?'

'It's him! He's here!' Anthea turned away from the sink, horrified. The flat was on the first floor, its kitchen window overlooked the car park at the back of the building—and she had just spotted a man getting out of a Rolls.

'Paul?'

'No, you idiot. Him!'

Gail looked delighted. 'Oh. *Him*. How nice! So I will get to meet him.'

'Now listen, Gail. There's no time to—just answer the

buzzer, tell him I've gone shopping. Don't let him get inside the building.'

'Aw, Anthea!'

'*Do it.*'

'All right, all right.' The buzzer had already sounded. Gail moved swiftly in to the living-room, Anthea on her heels, and pressed the button on the intercom. 'Hello? Who?' She turned to look at the younger girl, grinning from ear to ear. 'Russell? Oh, *Aden* Russell. Yes, Anthea's here, come right up.'

Anthea stood, impotent, powerless. Gail had already pressed the button which would open the doors downstairs. 'So much for security. I'll never forgive you for this, Gail Brennan. Judas!'

Gail was unmoved. 'You'd better drag a comb through your hair. He'll be up here in a jiff. I'll put the kettle on, I'll just have time for a cup of coffee before I go.'

Furious, Anthea headed for the door. There was no time for combing hair, no time for getting dressed. She was wearing her old sheepskin slippers, a housecoat she'd had for four years, her hair was a riot of tangled, shoulder-length curls—but so what? She swung the front door open before he had time to knock, her voice sugary sweet as she greeted him. 'Why, Aden! How lovely to see you again! Do come in.'

His face broke into a smile. 'Couldn't wait, eh?' He stepped inside, his eyes moving slowly over her from top to toe. 'Well, you're looking . . . different. Who's your clothes designer, Christian Dior?'

'No, Marks and Spencers. Do sit down and make yourself at home. Oh, this is Gail Brennan, my flat-mate. She and I work at the same hospital. Gail's a nurse, as you can see.'

'I was just about to have a cup of coffee before I go off to work. Will you have one, Mr Russell?'

'Aden, please. Thanks. No sugar, no milk.' He lowered his large frame into an armchair, keeping his attention on Gail. 'I'm sorry you'll have to dash off.'

'It's a hard life.' She shrugged and headed for the kitchen. All three of them knew he wasn't at all sorry.

The moment Gail left for the hospital, Anthea got down to business. 'So? Why are you here?'

'I told you last night, I want to talk to you about Sybil. And I don't mean her health.'

Anthea shrugged. 'Well, since you're here, get on with it.'

She hadn't meant to sound so rude, she really hadn't. It was the things Gail had said that were bothering her most, that were bothering her more than his arrival, actually. 'I'm sorry,' she said quickly. 'Really. It's just—perhaps we should try again, pretend we never met five years ago.'

'Five—what's that got to do with anything? You're being ridiculous about all that, Anthea. You were just a kid, and if I upset you, I'm sorry. That's hardly my fault, so stop holding it against me. Look, I'm here for a very good reason. Believe me, I'd rather be with my aunt. She doesn't know I've come to talk to you. You jumped to the wrong conclusion last night, which is my fault. I should have said that I wanted to talk about Sybil *and* you.'

'I'm not sure what you mean.'

'I mean this friendship of yours. It strikes me as odd. My aunt is over seventy and you're—very young.'

'I'm twenty-four. So?'

'So what's it all about?'

That's when he lost her, completely. 'Now hang on, am

I to infer that you're asking *why* your aunt and I are fond of each other?'

'No.' He was dead serious. 'I'm asking why you're fond of her.'

'But I don't see——'

'So much so,' he interrupted, 'that you're willing to go on holiday with her.'

'Willing? Honoured, more like. Oh, I know the villa belongs to you but it's nice of Sybil to want me as a companion.'

'It seems I'd better use words of one syllable.' He sighed, crossed one long leg over the other and fixed her with eyes that were neutral now, telling her nothing. 'Why should a beautiful young woman want to go alone on holiday with my maiden aunt, an eccentric old lady who'll spend most of her time dozing?'

It dawned, finally. Appalled, Anthea shot to her feet, her face a mask of fury. She could hardly breathe, she was so disgusted. 'Are you suggesting there's something about my friendship with Sybil that's . . . abnormal?'

For a split second he merely stared at her, his expression blank. Then he exploded, swearing loudly. 'Bloody hell! You can't really be that stupid! If you ever make another crack like that I'll give you the walloping you deserve. Now *sit down*.'

She sat, stunned, shocked at his fury and shocked at herself. What on earth had she been thinking about? It was too ridiculous, he couldn't possibly have thought . . . 'I'm sorry. It was just——'

The phone rang.

Anthea let it ring a couple of times before answering. It was Sybil. She greeted her normally enough, still looking at Aden as she spoke. '. . . it was a lovely party.

And how are you today, Sybil?'

Aden signalled her, shaking his head. Anthea nodded in acquiescence. Sybil had just told her that Aden had gone into Guildford, to the shops. She wouldn't contradict. 'And I'm ringing to ask you to dinner tonight, Anthea. It'll be just the three of us.'

Being careful not to let Aden see, Anthea crossed her fingers before lying. 'Oh, I'm sorry, I can't! I—have a date tonight.'

Sybil was both pleased and sorry. 'Oh! Well, that's nice. Anyone I know? But never mind, come to lunch tomorrow instead.'

'I——' Tomorrow was Sunday. Lunch. How could she get out of that? Was there any point in trying, really? 'That'll be lovely. What time do you want me . . .?'

Noon, was the answer. She put the phone down, sat down and conveyed the news to her visitor. 'I'm invited to lunch tomorrow.'

He hadn't forgiven her, he was still angry. 'So I gathered. And you couldn't manage dinner tonight because you have a date.' He paused, scrutinising her. 'So there is a man in your life.'

Anthea looked at her hands, wondering how she was going to get rid of him. She was going to ignore his last remark, it was none of his damned business anyway. 'Right, let's see if this will satisfy you: I meet a great number of people in my work, most of whom are very ordinary and uninteresting. I don't mean that unkindly, I mean most people tell me their troubles and talk about their ailments. Naturally. But not Sybil. I find her charming. And courageous and spirited and interesting. I love listening to her, I've never met anyone quite like her. Does that answer your question?'

'As far as it goes.'

She threw up her hands. 'What's that supposed to mean?'

'It means,' he said coldly, 'that it satisfies my curiosity as far as it goes. But is there more, I ask myself? Are there any other ways in which my aunt interests you? After all, she is a very rich old lady who's already suffered one stroke ...'

Anthea was much quicker on the uptake this time. And, this time, she didn't misunderstand him. 'Get out of here.' It was no more than a whisper. 'Get out of my home this minute! How dare you accuse me——'

'I accused you of nothing.' He got to his feet slowly, looking down at her.

'Out!' she shouted. 'Get out!'

'If you insist ...' He was already walking away from her. She hurtled out of the chair and chased after him. Why let him get away with it so easily? 'Just a minute!'

Aden turned to face her, both eyebrows raised sardonically. 'Something else on your mind?'

'There certainly is. For the record, I had no idea your aunt was rich. How could I have known? Why should I? There's nothing about her house or its contents which point to her being rich. Good grief, I've been thinking *you* subsidised her—her pension or something. I thought you were well off. I mean——'

'I know what you mean.'

'No, you don't!'

'You can calm down now. You're forgiven.'

She nearly screamed at that. 'Forgiven? I haven't done anything!'

'Then I owe you an apology, don't I?' He leaned against the front door, shrugging. 'I hereby apologise.'

Anthea almost laughed. Almost. 'Correct me if I'm wrong, but aren't you Sybil's favourite nephew? And aren't you her only relative in this country, one who fusses over her and makes damned sure he visits regularly?'

It didn't work. He merely looked blank. 'Correct. What are you getting at?'

'You know full well what I'm getting at. It's *you*, you're the gold-digger!'

He still looked blank. 'What gold is that?'

'Your aunt's, of course, you can stop looking so vacant and you can stop insulting my intelligence. I've seen through you. It's you who'll inherit Sybil's wealth, and you're here to warn me off, you're afraid she might leave me some money. Well, that is *not* my reason for befriending her and I am *not* going to stop seeing her just to satisfy you.'

'No, no, you've got it all wrong, Anthea. You see, I lied. Sybil isn't rich at all.'

Anthea's mouth fell open. For a moment she was speechless. 'You're crazy,' she accused. 'You're more than devious, you're nuts!'

'Have you quite finished?'

'I've finished.' Except that she was furious, except that she wanted to hit him.

'Then I'll go,' he said, and left.

It took Anthea a long time to get over that visit. It took days. She got through lunch on the Sunday for Sybil's sake, and that alone. It was Gail who took the brunt of her anger. Several times. By the following Wednesday, she had heard enough.

'Anthea, will you please try to forget all that? He wanted to see how you'd react, he was testing you——'

'I'm aware of that! How dare he? If he——'

'If he knew you, he wouldn't have needed to test you. *We* know that. But he doesn't. I can see his point of view, even if you can't. He was simply protecting his aunt, to his way of thinking. He would hardly be a gold-digger himself, even if there were some to dig. He must make a fortune in his profession, he's a hot-shot barrister. His picture was on the news last night.' Gail paused, presumably expecting Anthea, who rarely watched the news or read the papers, to be impressed. She wasn't. Gail went on, 'He's involved in that case which has been going on for weeks at——'

'I'm not interested.' Anthea had never actually thought for a moment that Aden's motives for keeping an eye on his aunt were the wrong ones. Firstly his fondness for Sybil was plain for anyone to see, secondly he couldn't be short of money, as Gail rightly pointed out. But he had been suspicious of Anthea, he still was.

She started clearing the table, still complaining. 'What right has he to test me, to suspect my motives? How *dare* he? I just can't describe how angry I feel inside, Gail.'

'You don't need to. You've been like a different person since last Saturday. I think I preferred you as you were, your increasing stuffiness and all. You fancy Aden, and I don't blame you, and you wanted him to have a good opinion of you. *Wait*, I haven't finished yet——'

'I've heard enough, thank you. More than enough. I shan't mention his name to you again. All right?' Anthea was near to tears. She couldn't work out what was happening, why Gail was so unsympathetic these days, why she didn't seem to understand anything. Of course she'd wanted Aden's good opinion of her, but only because he was Sybil's beloved nephew. He'd had the wrong impression of her to begin with. Years ago he'd thought her scatty and incompetent, now he thought her insincere.

She walked out of the room, slamming the door behind her. A part of her wanted to cancel her ticket to Tenerife next week, to explain to Sybil that she wouldn't be visiting her again. But she couldn't do that. Sybil would be terribly hurt. Besides, why the hell should she? And it would serve only to make Aden Russell believe the worst. She stripped off her clothes and headed for the shower, thinking of him now with hatred.

Ten minutes later she pulled on a pair of red cords and a thick white sweater. The December weather was getting colder daily. A flurry of snow was falling when she headed for the garages in the parking area at the back of the building. She turned the car heater on full blast but it hadn't warmed up properly by the time she reached Sybil's, which was only a short drive away.

'Oh, no!' Anthea switched off the engine and sat, looking despairingly at the vehicle outside Sybil's front door. Aden was here again. For how long? She hoped desperately he wasn't here for the evening. Maybe he'd just called in to say hello. She braced herself for the inevitable clash, not that he would be openly rude to her in front of his aunt. But it made no difference, his very courtesy had aggravated her the previous Sunday.

It was he who opened the door. He did so with a wide sweep, an exaggerated bow, a smile which would have melted the likes of Gail. 'Good evening, Anthea, welcome to you! You're looking gorgeous, as ever. What ensemble have we tonight?' he went on, reaching to help her out of her coat. 'Ah! Smart casual, I believe they call it?'

'I can manage, thank you.' She moved away from him, bristling. 'I hadn't expected to see you here.'

'You never know your luck, do you?' He was doing it again, flashing that smile of his, letting his eyes roam over her. If he was trying to make her feel self-conscious, he was succeeding. 'It's Scrabble for three tonight. I'll bet you can't wait!'

Anthea lifted her head. 'As a matter of fact I enjoy a game of Scrabble. Some people take pleasure in the simple things of life, but what would you know about that?' She didn't wait for an answer, she headed for the den.

An arm came around her waist, stopping her in her tracks. It also made her breath catch in her throat. The contact was shocking, abhorrent. She wished fervently that this man would not feel at liberty to put his hands on her. 'We're in the drawing-room this evening,' he said, turning her round. 'As for the simple things in life, are you one of them, Anthea? If so I could take pleasure in you, a great deal of it.'

As an example of the back-handed compliment, it was superb. She swore at him. It made not the slightest difference. He merely laughed, he laughed so loudly it had Sybil calling out to them. 'What's the joke? What are you two doing out there?'

Aden had an answer at the ready. 'I'm flirting with Anthea,' he said, his hand under her elbow as he steered her into the drawing-room. 'But she doesn't seem to appreciate it.'

Sybil peered over the spectacles she wore whenever she was reading or viewing. They spent most of the time resting on her bosom dangling from the chains they were attached to. 'Hard luck,' she told her nephew. 'Hello,

Anthea darling. I've had a lovely afternoon. Russ had a few hours free and he took me out for a drive. We had an early dinner and then we had a game of Scrabble, so we're warmed up and eager for more. I hope you play?'

'I certainly do.' Anthea sat in the rather battered leather armchair near the fire, facing Sybil. 'How are you, Sybil? You look a bit peaky, I hope Aden didn't tire you today.'

'I'm *fine*,' came the firm reply. Sybil always said that. 'Oh, while I think about it—Russ is going to collect us and take us to the airport next week.'

Anthea turned to him then. He was at the drinks cabinet, pouring a Scotch. 'There's really no need for you to go to such trouble. I have a car and——'

'And you don't want all the hassle of parking at Heathrow, or the unnecessary expense. It's no trouble, I live quite near the airport so it won't put me out. Honestly!' he added. 'Anyone would think you were trying to avoid my company, Anthea!'

'Don't be silly,' said Sybil, before the younger woman could make a retort.

'By the way,' Aden went on. 'I've been meaning to ask you, Anthea, how your holiday is going to affect your love life.'

She stared at him. 'I beg your pardon?'

'Your love life,' he said baldly. 'Won't your boyfriend object to your being away for two weeks?'

Again it was Sybil who spoke first, while Anthea was fuming, casting around for a suitable retort again.

'There is no man in Anthea's life,' she said, 'not that that's any of your business, Russ.'

'Too right,' Anthea muttered. All she wanted to do was go home, get out of his orbit. He was looking at her suspiciously now, no doubt thinking about the date she was supposed to have had last weekend.

He won at Scrabble. Both games, quickly and hands down. Sybil suggested a third game, saying she wanted revenge, but Anthea declined. 'You two go ahead. I must go, I have to make an early start in the morning. Thursday's always the hardest day of the week. I'll be working with people in the gym first thing.'

'But it isn't ten o'clock yet——'

'And I have a few things to see to when I get home.'

'Very well, dear.' Sybil was about to add something but she changed her mind. 'Would you fetch Anthea's coat, Russ?'

'Of course.' He was already on his feet. No sooner was he out of earshot than Sybil went on, 'You don't like him, do you, Anthea? Perhaps you would rather avoid his company?'

Anthea felt awkward, very. What could she say? The last thing she wanted was to hurt Sybil. 'I—it isn't that I don't like him, exactly. It's—I think it's what people call a personality clash.'

'What's the difference?'

'The difference between what?' Aden was back.

'My young friend thinks you and she have what is called a personality clash.'

'Does she now?' He held Anthea's coat up for her, giving her no opportunity to refuse his help. 'Then we should do something about that. Maybe we should get to know one another better. I'll tell you what, Anthea, how about having dinner with me tomorrow or Friday? Just the two of us, all nice and cosy. We'll go into London and have a really——'

'I can't.' Anthea's answer came quickly, snappily, and

she was not contrite. He was putting her on the spot. Well, it wouldn't work, not any more. She was sick of being victimised by him.

'May I ask why?' he asked, while Sybil looked on benignly. She seemed more amused than anything else.

'Because I don't want to. I could say I have a lot of things to do before my holidays, which I have, but you'd recognise that as an excuse. So it's simpler to tell the truth, isn't it? I don't want to have dinner alone with you.'

Aden shrugged, looked directly at his aunt as if he were helpless. 'What can a man do?'

'Try harder.' She turned to Anthea. 'Goodnight, my dear. Will you be here for tea on Sunday? Around four? Russ won't be here.'

Anthea felt awful, guilty suddenly. 'I'd love it. I—goodnight, Sybil.' She bent down to kiss her, whispering, 'I'm sorry.'

'It's your privilege,' came the swift reply.

Nothing was said when Aden saw her out, much to her surprise. There was merely an exchange of goodnights. It gave Anthea a great deal of pleasure to realise she'd ruffled him. No doubt he wasn't used to having his dinner dates refused.

Her pleasure vanished as she stepped outside. She'd left her car lights on and she knew, somehow, that it wasn't going to start. Hers was one of those vehicles that coughed and got reluctant when it was left standing in wet weather. It was covered in snow now. She looked from the car to the closed door of the house. It was his fault, she thought illogically. She'd been so taken aback to see his Rolls there earlier, she'd forgotten to switch her lights off.

Five minutes later Aden was approaching her. He had his coat on. 'Having trouble?'

Anthea was still trying to start the engine. 'What does it sound like?'

'It sounds like you're having trouble.'

He was grinning, grinning! She ignored it. 'I—do you know anything about cars?'

'I'm a lawyer, not a mechanic. But I can tell you this much: you're not going to get it going, the battery's dead. In fact it sounds like rigor mortis has set in.'

She dropped the keys into her bag and got out. She wasn't going to ring the AA, not at this hour, she couldn't be bothered waiting around for them. She would ring a garage first thing in the morning. 'I'll ring for a taxi.'

'Don't be ridiculous, I'll drop you home.'

'I said I'll ring a taxi.' She walked away from him, heading for the house.

'Anthea!' Aden's voice, low but furious, stopped her. 'Dammit, what's the matter with you? You will not disturb Sybil, she's just gone up to bed.'

'Oh. I—thought you were having another game.'

'We changed our minds.' He pointed to the Rolls, his tone unaltered. 'Get in.'

'No.' She pulled her coat more closely around her, wiped a snowdrop off her nose and turned away from him. 'I'll walk. It's not that far to——'

He moved like lightning, startling her. Both arms came around her waist this time and she suddenly found herself clean off the ground. He carried her the few yards to his car, dumped her firmly on her feet, flung the passenger door open and glared at her. 'The choice is yours: either I throw you in or you get in the normal way.'

She got in. He ranted all the way. It took only a few

minutes to get to Anthea's flat but not once did he stop. While she was called stupid and stubborn, unreasonable and illogical, worse than the average female, whatever that meant, irritating—nay, *infuriating*—she said not a word. She kept her head averted towards the window and said nothing at all, though she was just as angry as he was.

When he came to a halt at the back of the building, she tried immediately to open the door. She couldn't. Well, it was a Rolls Royce, no doubt there was some magic control switch somewhere. 'Unlock the door,' she demanded.

'When I'm ready.' He was looking up at her flat. 'There are no lights on. I take it Gail's out?'

'She's on nights at the moment. Unlock the door, damn you!'

He pressed a button, got out himself and was standing by her side before she'd even straightened up. 'I think a little sorting out is in order. We'll do it over a cup of coffee.'

Anthea could hardly breathe. It was freezing outside but she felt hot, hot and frustrated beyond speech. It was no use, she knew. He would have his way. She set off in the direction of her flat with him at her heels—as if he expected her to turn round and bolt.

She flung open her front door, flicked the lights on, strode through to the living-room and flung her bag on to the settee. She flung herself on to it, too. 'You can whistle for the coffee. Just say what you want to say and then go.'

Aden didn't say anything for several minutes. He shrugged out of the sheepskin he was wearing, draped it over the back of the settee and sat in an armchair, at right-angles to her. At length, very quietly, he said,

'Would you mind telling me what you have against me, Anthea?'

She sighed. The day, the evening, had caught up with her. She was tired suddenly, very tired. 'You hurt me,' she said wearily. 'And I'm not about to forgive you for that.'

'Hurt you? But how? You don't mean—you're not still going on about that episode in the past, are you?'

'No, of course not,' she snapped. 'I'm talking about last Saturday. Here. Your accusations.'

'I didn't make any.'

'Your implications then.'

He inclined his head. 'Look, don't blame me for that. I'm overly protective of Sybil, I know. I can't help it, Anthea. She's very dear to me, as she was to my mother, whom I adored. She's the last one of that generation of the family and I worry about her—more than she realises.'

Anthea listened as he talked. His words were getting to her and she didn't look at him, didn't want to consider for a moment that he'd been justified in suspecting her in any way at all.

'I worry about her health,' he went on, 'about her happiness and, yes, the people she chooses to mix with. And I didn't know you, did I? I'd met you but I didn't know what sort of person you were. I do now, and I'm sorry. If I hurt you, I apologise. It was just that I couldn't see why you and she—but you explained that.'

'And I shouldn't have needed to.'

'And you shouldn't have needed to,' he agreed. 'In fact that was an insult to both of you.' He was taking the wind out of her sails, making it harder for her to remain angry.

She looked at him, her eyes narrowing. 'You're very

clever, Aden Russell. Your tactics are admirable. I suppose it's your training as a lawyer. I shouldn't like to be cross-examined by you.'

He didn't answer for a moment. He merely held her eyes, his clear green gaze gauging her. 'That was pretty pointless, Anthea. We're not trying to score off one another, are we? Either you accept my apology or you don't.'

'I accept it,' she sighed. 'But it doesn't change how I feel about you. I find you arrogant, facetious and offensive.' She held up her hand, stopping his protest. 'But I do accept your apology, if only because it makes life easier.'

'I'd hoped for more than that.' It was he who sounded weary now. He got to his feet. 'I'd hoped you'd recognise it was really meant. I hoped you'd meet me half-way, if only for Sybil's sake.'

Why Anthea capitulated, she didn't know. 'I—all right.' He was reaching for his coat, and the strain between them hung heavily on the air. 'All right, Aden, we'll start again. I'll make some coffee and we'll try, for fifteen minutes or so, to talk to one another as if we've just met. How's that for compromise?'

'Sounds good to me . . .'

Sybil was told about that conversation the following evening, after Anthea collected her car. She had woken to find herself on a more even keel, more like her usual self, and was gratified to find the snow had vanished. She took a taxi to the hospital and found her car working by the time she got to the garage near Sybil's late in the afternoon. She popped in with the intention of staying only half an hour, ended up staying to dinner and, inevitably, Aden was mentioned—by Sybil initially.

'You know, he might be very dear to me but I'm not blind to his faults, Anthea. He's cynical in general and in particular about women. Maybe he's afraid he'll fall for one some day—in fact, I'm sure he is. He's attracted to them more than he's repelled but he's a suspicious devil at the best of times, he says he can see through women, he thinks they're devious and cunning. Which we are!'

Anthea laughed, she couldn't help it, Sybil was chuckling so hard at her final statement. 'Don't exaggerate, Sybil! Maybe he has reason to be cynical?' she ventured. 'I mean, maybe he's been hurt or let down or something?'

Sybil blinked. 'Not to my knowledge. Not that he tells me everything. I know he's had an endless string of women, he's even brought some to meet me, over the years. But he's never got really serious about one, more's the pity.'

'Why is it a pity?'

There was a shrug. 'You're right to pick me up on that. I said it for purely selfish reasons. I'm never going to have grandchildren around me—it would be nice to have the next best thing, though.'

Aden's children. Russell's children. 'He must be happy as he is.'

'I don't doubt that,' Sybil agreed. 'He has everything he wants, a busy social life, a nice house and car, his work—which he loves. And he has all the women he wants, regardless of what he thinks of them as a whole. But we've digressed, Anthea. You apologised to me last night and there was no need. You're perfectly entitled not to like Russ, I wouldn't have you pretending to just to keep me happy. In any case,' she added, her smile mischievous, 'I knew. I knew it the night you met here. I don't know what happened between you in the past, but whatever it was, you hadn't forgiven him.'

'Well, I have now,' Anthea announced. 'It was something and nothing, a silly business really. He called it teasing and I was so sensitive in those days, I couldn't take it.'

'You were younger.'

'Quite. As a matter of fact, I had a pleasant chat with him when he drove me home last night.'

'Really?'

Anthea smiled inwardly. The old lady's reaction, her obvious pleasure at the news, confirmed what she was basically sure of. Sybil was perfectly capable of coping with any antipathy between her nephew and her friend ... but she would obviously find things easier, pleasanter, if it didn't exist. That was one reason Anthea was making an effort now. The other reason was that her anger really had diminished. Somehow, Aden had managed to redeem himself a little last night.

'Well?' she asked. 'Are you going to tell me about it, Anthea? Or was it personal?'

'No, it wasn't personal.' Hardly. In fact her chat with Aden had almost been like a game, a game of questions and answers. An exchange of opinions on matters strictly neutral. She wanted to laugh about it now. 'We were talking about our respective jobs and then about the government—there was common ground there, you'll be pleased to learn. We're both of the same mind.'

Sybil looked at her as if she hadn't seen her before. 'Good lord, how very boring! You needn't bother telling me any more, thank you. Still, I suppose it was a start . . .'

CHAPTER FOUR

ANTHEA stood by the kitchen window. Aden and Sybil weren't due for another ten minutes but she had been ready for the past half hour. Everything was done, packed, her passport was in her handbag, a note of farewell to Gail was propped up against the kettle.

There was nothing left to do. She looked up at the sky, dark and ominous as if filled with snow. It was only two o'clock in the afternoon but it was like twilight. 'Don't let it snow,' she said aloud. Their flight wasn't until four-thirty and she wanted no delays, no hitches to the start of their holiday.

She did a mental check on the contents of her vanity case. Most contingencies were covered, it was like a miniature chemist's shop, there was everything in there from sun-creams to Savlon. The contents of her suitcase were mainly new, clothes she had shopped for especially. She had gone in to London on Saturday and spent the day. Searching for summer clothes and bikinis in December had been fun.

Spotting Aden's car coming to a halt, she felt a ripple of excitement. It wouldn't be long now, before she was winging her way to warm weather and a nice rest. Sybil didn't get out of the Rolls, Aden got out, gave Anthea a wave and was walking into her flat a few moments later.

'Hello, Anthea. All organised and ready?'

'Absolutely. I was just taking a look at the weather, looks like we're in for more snow.'

'That isn't a worry. There's no snow in London but it's quite foggy, at least it was when I left.'

'You've been in court today?'

'All morning.' He picked up her suitcase and gave an exaggerated grunt. 'My God—what have you got in here, gold bars?'

'Just a few.'

He put the case down again, grinning. 'How long are you thinking of staying in Tenerife?'

He was still joking. He knew precisely how long she'd be there. Fourteen days. It was what she thought of as good timing: she would leave on the Tuesday and he would arrive on the Wednesday. 'There's nothing in my suitcase which isn't a necessity,' she told him.

'If you say so. Speaking of necessities, have you got your driving licence?'

She had, an international one she'd got especially. Sybil had told her Aden had a car in Tenerife, one she would be at liberty to use. 'But I won't be using your car, I don't think it's fair to; I have no experience of driving on the wrong side of the road and I don't want the responsibility of using someone else's car. I thought I might hire one—after Sybil and I have spent a few days lazing around.'

'That's crazy. My car's fully insured for any driver. When friends of mine stay at the villa they always use the car, that's what it's there for. And don't worry about being on the wrong side of the road, the traffic isn't exactly hectic and you'll soon get the hang of it.'

Anthea didn't argue the point. It was kind of him but—well, she'd see. She picked up her vanity case, slung her voluminous handbag over her shoulder, and they left.

The nearer they drove towards London, the foggier it

got. Sybil, too, was concerned about possible delays. 'I shall hate hanging around the airport. Heaven knows I've done enough of that in my time, I'm too old for it now.'

'Now don't start worrying,' Aden told her. 'There are still clear patches here and there. Things can change drastically in a couple of hours. If there happens to be a long delay, I'll take you back to my place for a while, where you'll be comfortable. All right, darling?'

When there was no answer Anthea turned round to look at her. Sybil was sitting in the back of the Rolls, queen-like, wearing a full-length sable coat whose age it was impossible to tell. She winked at Anthea. 'You're a good boy, Russ.'

He muttered something unintelligible, glanced at Anthea and started grinning. 'Did you hear that? I'm thirty-six years old, and she'll be saying it when I'm sixty-six.'

'Of course I will,' Sybil laughed. 'After all, I'll be entitled, I'll be a hundred and three by then.'

'You'll probably make it, too. I'll have to put up with you all that time.'

Aden briefed them on what they could expect when they got to Tenerife. There was a married couple who looked after the villa in his absence, which Anthea knew already, and they, or at least one of them, would be waiting at the airport to collect them. 'Lucia will do the cleaning and cooking but I suggest you do your own shopping for food and make it clear how you want it cooked.'

'I take it she speaks English?' Anthea asked, alarmed. She had a reasonable command of French but only about two words of Spanish.

'They both do. Her husband is Pedro, by the way. Peter to you.'

Anthea smiled. 'And why can't Lucia be trusted to shop? Does she spend too much?'

'No, on the contrary, she's very economical. To a fault. She'd present you with all sorts of weird and wonderful concoctions if you gave her free rein. Still, perhaps you like garlic with everything?'

'I'm fairly adventurous . . .' she said, meeting his glance, '. . . when it comes to food. Aden, will you keep your attention on the road, please?' Just because she was feeling happy there was no need to go overboard. A truce had been called, her anger with him had faded away but her dislike of this man had not diminished one iota.

There were delays. An announcement was made that their plane would take off two hours late just after Anthea and Sybil had checked in at the airport. Aden was still with them, he'd put his car in the short-term car park.

'That means we'll take off at six-thirty,' said Sybil, sighing. 'And get there at about ten—or is there a time difference? Anyway, it's an awful bore!'

Aden slipped an arm around her shoulders. 'I know, darling. Come on, let's get ourselves a cup of coffee. Two hours, it isn't worth going away and coming back.'

Sybil agreed, nodded as if she'd just made a decision and drew herself up to her full height. 'Then we must keep as cheerful as we can. Will the bar be open?'

Anthea blinked. 'You're not thinking of getting drunk, are you?'

'I might,' came the defiant answer. 'But later, perhaps. All right, I'll settle for coffee in the meantime.'

Several cups later the fog had thickened and they all

knew, before the announcement was made, what was going to happen. The airport was closed for the night.

'Right, that's it. Come along, ladies, I shall deposit you near the doors and fetch the car. We'll go home.'

'To Guildford?'

'To my home. We'll ring the airport first thing tomorrow and find out what's happening. Unfortunately I won't be able to bring you back here myself, I have to be in chambers early. We'll have to book a taxi to collect you from my place. Don't look so perturbed, Anthea, you'll be perfectly comfortable.'

She wasn't perturbed, she was disappointed. Still, it could have been worse—some people would be sleeping on the floor in the airport tonight. She thought again about the contents of her vanity case, which she'd kept as hand-luggage. There was no change of clothing in it but at least she had her toiletries. Her suitcase had gone through the usual channels from the check-in desk; she only hoped that the inevitable chaos in the airport wouldn't result in its disappearance.

Aden's house was impressive. It took almost an hour to get there although it wasn't far from Heathrow. It was in Hayes, Middlesex. It was detached, standing in what appeared to be large gardens. The fog was so bad, it was difficult to tell, especially with the house being in darkness.

Aden went from room to room, switching on lights. The interior of the house was, as Anthea had expected, both graceful and masculine, the light fittings and furniture of the traditional type. The decorations and curtains were without fuss and the carpeting was chocolate brown throughout except, of course, for the kitchen, which she saw last. Having been shown to guest rooms by Aden, both women tidied themselves up and rejoined him in the drawing-room for a drink.

'We have a slight problem,' he told them. 'My housekeeper has prepared dinner as usual—but only for one. She comes in every afternoon,' he added for Anthea's benefit.

'So what's——' She broke off as the telephone rang.

Aden excused himself and picked it up. It was within arm's reach of where he was sitting, 'Aden Russell. Hello, Fiona, this is . . . something gone wrong?' There was a pause, a long pause, interspersed only by his, 'I see.' After a few more minutes he said, 'I'm sorry, love. Yes, I know. If it weren't so foggy I'd suggest you came over right now, but it's impossible.'

At the sudden softening of his voice, Anthea looked around the room, not wishing to eavesdrop but unable to prevent it. Sybil was doing so openly, watching her nephew with interest. Whoever Fiona was, she was talking ten to the dozen and Aden was concerned about her. Again he said, 'I see,' then, 'We'll discuss it thoroughly tomorrow. What time will you be in—assuming the weather's cleared?'

He put the phone down. 'Sorry about that.'

'Fiona?' Sybil's eyebrows had risen. 'The Fiona I've met, the one from your chambers? Fiona Calveley?'

'That's right.' To Anthea he added, 'A colleague.'

'Another barrister,' Sybil enlarged. 'Belongs to the same chambers as Russ. It sounded as if she had a problem, darling.'

'She has.'

'A professional one?'

'I think that's enough fishing, Sybil!'

Anthea suppressed a smile at the older woman's

curiosity. She was curious herself but wouldn't dream of showing it. So the phone call had been from a colleague. A colleague and—anything else? When had Sybil met Fiona Calveley? In chambers? Hardly. Sybil never went in to London.

'Now then,' Aden was saying, 'where were we? Ah yes, about our problem—our dinner.'

'Why is it a problem?' Anthea asked. 'Are your cupboards bare?'

'Far from it. I've got a fridge, a freezer and several cupboards full of food, thanks to my housekeeper. She looks after me very well, actually.'

Anthea smiled inwardly. No wonder he didn't want a wife. He hardly needed one, did he? It was quite obvious he lived like a lord. 'But you can't cook. Is that it?'

'Got it in one. Of course you wouldn't have expected that of me, would you? My talents lie in other realms.'

'I can cook,' she said. 'It happens to be one of my talents. Problem solved. It'll be my pleasure.'

'I was hoping you'd say that.'

'No, Aden, you knew very well I'd say that.'

'My, my,' Sybil put in. Her head had been moving from one direction to another, like one at a tennis match. 'It's better than television, watching you two.'

'It is fun, isn't it?' Aden agreed, though he didn't take his eyes from the younger woman. 'I rather like this, having Anthea captive for the night.'

It was quite late by the time they finally sat down to eat, later than was usual for Sybil. She was half asleep before they'd finished and excused herself immediately afterwards. 'Forgive me, I can't stay up a moment longer. All that excitement and then the let down—you don't mind if I leave you to clear away, Anthea?'

'Of course not.' She covered Sybil's hand and gave it a little squeeze. 'Aden will help me.'

'I'm sure he's very good at putting things in dishwashers. It's just as well he has one of those contraptions—of his talents which lie in other realms I'm sure washing pots by hand isn't one of them.'

It was more than Anthea could do to stop herself laughing. Sybil Manly-Smythe didn't miss a thing. 'Shall I see you upstairs, Sybil? Do you need any help?'

Aden closed his eyes, put both hands over his ears as if waiting for an explosion. It came. 'Since when?' Sybil demanded. 'If the day comes when I can't get out of my own clothes, I'll—I'll—well, I don't know what I'll do!'

Aden had a suggestion. 'We'll hire some gorgeous male nurse to do it for you.' Sybil rose haughtily from the table and vanished, not in the least amused. Apparently.

'I think you just went too far,' Anthea said, not quite certain about Sybil.

'Not at all, she loves being teased. You can't shock Sybil, don't you know that by now?'

'I've never tried to shock her, wouldn't dream of it,' she said truthfully. He was still laughing, keeping her eyes drawn to him because this was a side of Aden Russell she'd never seen before. It was as if years had fallen away from him, the grey at his temples looked quite incongruous just now. 'Well,' she heard herself saying, 'if that's what laughter does for you, you should try it more often.'

He sobered somewhat. 'Explain.'

Anthea was already wishing she hadn't said it. 'There's no need to look suspicious, it was a compliment, actually.'

'From you? From you to me? I'd have thought it

beyond the realms of possibility, beyond one's wildest——'

'Oh, shut up!' In her embarrassment Anthea got to her feet and started collecting dishes. As soon as everything was cleared and the dishwasher was whirring, she said she was going to bed.

There was a protest. 'You can't be serious? It isn't ten o'clock yet, not quite.'

Anthea had her back to him, she was rinsing the dishcloth, having wiped the work surfaces. 'We're all hoping for an early start tomorrow, remember?'

From behind her the voice said, 'Come into the drawing-room and have a nightcap with me.'

She shrugged, turning, smiling, walking away ... 'Thanks, but no thanks.'

'I won't allow you to run away from me. That's what it amounts to.'

Irritated, she stopped and turned to face him. Aden was leaning against the cooker, looking totally out of place in his own kitchen. His dark pinstripe suit was as immaculate as it had been when he'd put in on that morning and the only thing which denoted he was at leisure were the open buttons at his neck, his tie shoved to one side. Calmly, quietly, she asked, 'Now why should I want to run away from you?'

'Suppose you tell me,' he said smoothly. 'We've had our differences but——'

'You're wrong there, we *have* our differences.'

'I thought we'd sorted them out? I thought we'd called a truce?'

'We have, but we still have our differences. Differences of another nature.' She was speaking reasonably, having no wish to let this grow into an argument. All she wanted was to be truthful. 'I'm too tired to play questions and answers tonight, Aden. You see, basically I have nothing to say to you, nor you to me, I'm sure. To be honest I'd find it hard work, sitting alone with you over a drink.'

'Your choice of words fascinates me.' He was standing perfectly still, only his eyes were moving and they were roaming over her in a way that had become familiar to her. It was bothering her now as much as it always had. No, it was bothering her more now.

He was moving towards her. 'Differences of another nature,' he repeated. 'Would you care to elucidate? Suppose you tell me what's going through your mind right now.'

His nearness was intimidating. He was towering over her, standing within arm's length, his eyes narrowed slightly as if monitoring her reactions, as if determined to discover her thoughts. She lifted her head. 'I should have thought it plain enough, it means that basically we have nothing in common.'

'Ah, but that's where you're wrong. We have at least one thing in common, one that we know about. There's probably a whole lot more but you won't open up and allow me to find out about those.'

'Aden,' she said patiently, 'I haven't the faintest idea what you're talking about.'

'Don't lie to me, Anthea.'

'Sybil told me you have a convoluted mind. You've lost me.'

'Then allow me to help you find yourself, Anthea.' He smiled, reaching for her before she could guess his intention.

It was only as his arms closed about her that she

reacted, struggling, hissing at him. 'Don't *do* that! How many times——' She got no farther. Aden took not the slightest notice of her protests, he never had. Worse, he was kissing her, his mouth had claimed hers forcefully, harshly, with a determination that overwhelmed and overpowered her. But she was still struggling, trying desperately to wrench free. She couldn't, she was pinned between him and the wall, both of which were equally unyielding, equally impossible to move. And his kiss went on . . . and on.

Quite suddenly it changed, he changed. He did not break the contact of his mouth, he lessened its pressure, letting her breathe. He shifted his stance, too, moving his body fractionally away from her. In other words she could have broken free then . . . but she didn't. By then it was too late, it was more than she could do, more than she even wanted to do.

It was Aden who called a halt. He moved back a little more, putting both hands lightly on her shoulders as she stood, her breasts rising and falling as she fought to breathe normally. She was glad of the wall behind her now, it was supporting her. Her legs seemed to have lost all their strength.

'I think I've made myself clear,' he said softly, his eyes locked on to hers. His were not in the least amused, hers were wide with alarm. 'I think I've made my point. This is what we have in common, Anthea. The one thing we both know about.'

It happened again, with a difference. When his arms slid around her waist, her arms went around his neck, as if they had a will of their own, were not under her control. Her body was acting independently of her brain, it was enjoying the feel of him, the length of his body pressing against her.

It was only when he raised his head and spoke to her, finally, that she returned to normal, that she could co-ordinate. 'You wouldn't deny it now, Angel Face?'

Anthea lowered her eyes, wanting to weep. No, she couldn't deny it. It was a little late for that. To say the least. It was all she could do to string a sentence together, to make him realise his victory was but a small one. She had to do that, she had to! With as much scorn as she could master, she tried. 'It doesn't change anything. I still have nothing to say to you and you can rest assured your name will never be on my party lists. Goodnight—give me a shout when you wake up in the morning.'

She walked away to the sound of his laughter, low laughter, disbelieving, infuriating laughter. He had the last word, his voice reached her just as she got to the stairs in the hall. 'I hope you sleep well, pretty one, but I doubt it. You should have had that drink with me, it wouldn't have been half as disturbing.'

How right he was! It was hours before she got to sleep, before she could stop tossing and turning in what seemed to be a very uncomfortable bed. How could she have let herself down like that? How could she have proved him right? Moreover, why hadn't she known in the first place, why hadn't she realised she was physically attracted to him? He'd known it. Gail had known it.

Maybe even Sybil knew it.

CHAPTER FIVE

'I THOUGHT we'd never get here, Anthea.'

'We're not there yet, not quite!' There was still the landing to go through, the plane was circling Tenerife now. It had been a long and tiring day. The morning had been as clear as a bell, typical of the contrariness of British weather which had cheated her out of a day of her holiday! As anticipated there had been delays, a backlog of departures to clear. Heathrow had been chaotic.

Anthea's mind had been chaotic, too. In spite of all the distractions and frustrations, she had been thinking about Aden almost constantly all day, with irritation mostly. She was glad to be away from him, well away. Now her destination was in sight she was re-energised, her tiredness falling away from her. Come the morning thoughts of Aden would have vanished, too. With luck.

'How nice to be young,' Sybil said, aware of Anthea's sudden buoyancy. 'I'm afraid I can't conjure up the same sort of energy, it's been a long day and all I want is my bed.'

Anthea smiled. When Sybil actually admitted to being tired, it meant she was tired. 'We'll soon be on *terra firma*. I suppose Lucia and Pedro will have thought to ring the airport, check what time we're due?'

'I most certainly hope so! If they're not there, we'll have to jump into a taxi.'

'Jump, Sybil?'

There was a chuckle. 'That's just the sort of thing Russ

66

would have done—picked me up on the word. I hope he isn't going to be a bad influence on you.'

He's already been a bad influence on me, Anthea thought. He had stirred in her something she hadn't felt since she'd been in love with Tony. Was that a bad thing? Anthea could almost hear Gail asking the question. 'What's wrong with that?' she'd say. 'It's about time you met a man who could, if you ask me.

The very thought of wanting someone worried Anthea, most especially the likes of Aden Russell. How, *how* could she be physically attracted to a man she didn't even like? She had asked herself the question a hundred times today, to no avail. She might as well try to explain the mysteries of black holes in space.

Their luggage arrived, looking a little battered but intact, much to Anthea's relief. Pedro was waiting for them, a short, rotund man of forty or so with black shiny hair and a moustache. In his hands he was holding a notice with Sybil's name on it—well, almost. It said 'Miss Syble Russell' but everyone knew what it meant. By the time they got into his car—or was it Aden's car?—he was calling Anthea 'An-thea,' because she told him to drop the 'Miss' and he was calling Sybil 'Mees Seeble' because she didn't invite him to drop the Miss.

'Lucia she waits at the house. She likes to have food ready when you get home. She is making not the big meal but a hot . . .' he broke off, hunting for a word. 'Supper. This is it, supper!'

Garlic with everything? Or would it be spiced Horlicks and a sandwich?

Out, Aden, get *out* of my mind!

Determinedly she fell into conversation with Pedro, wishing it were daylight so she could look at the scenery at the same time. 'Where is the villa, exactly? I know it's in the south of the island, but that's about all.'

'It is between Los Cristianos and the Costa del Silencio, the coast of silence. The north of Tenerife is greener, more ... pretty, but the beaches are volcanic and not good. Here in the south we have more sunshine and the better beaches. It is quiet here, I think you will like.' Pedro glanced at her, reconsidering. 'But you are young, if you want the night-life you must go in to Los Cristianos or La Playa de las Americas. There you will find the music and the clubs, the good fun and many happy people.'

Sybil said little on the drive to the villa, her eyelids were drooping and Anthea felt sorry for her. Sorry but not concerned. Apart from her obvious tiredness, she was looking well enough.

It was frustrating, not being able to see the scenery, the villa when Pedro told her they were turning on to the road which led to it. The road was bumpy, more like a track, and unlit. In the headlights of the car, Anthea could see it was white, though, even from some distance, its exterior smooth and clean. Lights were shining from most windows and there were several outside lamps around the building itself. In front of it, beyond a patio on which there were tables and chairs, was the swimming pool. Sybil had been right. It was big for a private pool. Anthea felt like jumping in there and then, it was twinkling seductively, lit from the base with lights shimmering beneath the water. It was certainly warm enough to swim in spite of the hour.

They drew to a halt on a driveway on which was parked an English car, a Triumph Spitfire. 'That is the car of Señor Russell,' Anthea was informed. 'It is pretty, yes?'

'Yes.' So it was. It was a comfort to know it was fully insured but—would she use it? She'd never driven a sports car before.

Even more so than it had when she'd stepped from the plane, the difference in the air struck Anthea as she got out of Pedro's car and she revelled in it, breathing it in appreciatively. It seemed scented but not with the fragrance of flowers. The nearest she could get to naming the scent was ... oranges. The air smelt vaguely of oranges! Or was it her imagination?

Sybil couldn't eat her supper. She was past eating, she said. She apologised to Lucia, who was the bubbly type, as dark-haired as her husband, as short as he, but slimmer.

'It was kind and thoughtful of you to have supper ready for us but I'm afraid I couldn't do it justice. No, don't look disappointed, dear. I'll make up for it tomorrow, you'll see.'

Lucia, placated, looked hopefully at Anthea. Sybil answered for her. 'Yes, my young friend will eat. She might even eat my share, too.'

Anthea laughed. She might at that, she felt hungry enough. 'I'll say goodnight then, Sybil. I don't suppose you'll want me to wake you in the morning?'

'No need,' came the cheery reply. 'I sleep little but often, it's a symptom of old age, so people tell me. I'll be up with the lark—if they have larks here.'

Anthea exchanged a few words with Lucia, whose English was very similar to that of her husband, while Pedro showed Sybil her room and brought in the luggage. 'I'm impressed by your English, Lucia. I wish my

Spanish were as good. All I can say is *"Si"* and *"No"*.'

The older girl grinned at that, her admiration for Anthea's appearance unhidden. She reached out and touched a lock of her pale blonde hair. 'Beautiful! Your hair, you, beautiful! *Señorita*, when one is as young and as beautiful as you, "no" can be the very important word.'

'Hmm.' Anthea agreed in part. She had never considered herself beautiful but Lucia's second statement was a valid one.

'Ahhh! This is a big problem for you. I think so.'

'Not exactly.' Anthea smiled, liking her already. 'But you never know, it might be one day.' Now why had she said that? She shook herself. 'About your English, do Spaniards learn it in school?'

She was admonished, gently. 'I am not a Spaniard, *señorita*. Neither is my Pedro. We are *Canarian*. I come from Gran Canaria,' she went on proudly, 'and Pedro was born here in Tenerife.'

'Canarian. Oh. I'm sorry.'

'An-thea? Shall I taking you to your room now?' Pedro was back, smiling, having heard the tail end of the conversation. 'Lucia has the pride in her island, as you see, but Tenerife is bigger and more beautiful.'

There was a sudden burst of Spanish, rapid, bouncing back and forth between the two. It went right over Anthea's head. It sounded like an argument but she knew better. 'Where do you two live? I mean, how far away?'

'A few kilometres. Four, five.'

'We have a big house. It is necessary because we have three children, an old uncle, one father and one grandfather who is very, very old. It is a nice house, not as nice as this one but it is nice.'

The villa was more than nice, it was splendid in Anthea's opinion. Unlike Aden's home, this place was very modern, its walls white, tiled floors scattered with rugs, all aimed at the illusion of coolness, though there was air-conditioning. It wasn't furnished Spanish-style at all, rather it was stainless steel and glass, the overstuffed sofas and armchairs beige, scattered with cushions for splashes of colour. The walls were dotted with paintings, originals by the look of it, and the lighting was achieved with various lamps and spotlights. It was immaculate and yet it was very much a place to relax in—which was precisely what Anthea intended to do.

She slept like a log that night. No sooner had her head touched the pillow than she was out for the count. The journey and everything that went with it had caught up with her.

She woke with a start in the morning, wondering where she was. She giggled, excited, flinging away the single sheet she'd covered herself with for the night. This—in December! It was marvellous, she couldn't wait to get out in the sun.

There was no one around when she emerged after her shower, or so she thought. Only then did she look at her watch, astonished. It was getting on for eleven, she'd slept for nearly twelve hours. 'I don't believe it!'

'Anthea?' Sybil's voice floated towards her, it was hard to tell from which direction.

'Where are you?'

'I'm out here, darling. On the veranda.'

Anthea followed the voice. There was Sybil, sitting in the shade on the veranda, her head covered with a flat, bright blue hat. 'Where did you get that thing? Why are you wearing it?'

'What? Oh. This. One can't be too careful, it's years since I've exposed myself to the sun.'

'You're hardly exposed, Sybil, you're fully dressed and sitting in the shade!'

'That's what I mean. I'll tell you what, though, I could get used to this. Nice, isn't it?' Her arms moved out in a wide, sweeping gesture.

Anthea stepped away from the villa and looked around, seeing for the first time where she was and what surrounded her. The sea was not in sight but she knew in which direction it was and that it wasn't far away, just over a hill, not quite in walking distance unless one was feeling particularly energetic. To the rear, at some distance, were more hills, much higher ones, beyond which lay Mount Teide, the volcanic mountain she had read about.

Several other villas were in sight, none of them crowding each other, not by a long way. It was a pretty, carefully thought out development of just a few luxury homes, nestling in a shallow valley through which the gentlest of breezes blew. The landscape here was dramatic: barren, dry, beaten by the sun. The sky was a perfect azure, cloudless, the gardens surrounding the villa and its pool were beautifully tended, dotted with palm trees and huge tubs of flowers overflowing in a riot of vivid colours. 'It's lovely,' she agreed. 'And I look forward to seeing the north of the island, Pedro said it's much greener.'

'I heard.' Sybil looked dubious. 'I can't promise to go with you, darling, I don't know that I could keep up with you, sightseeing. Oh, I do hope you won't be bored here with——'

'Sybil! Don't say it. Sightseeing would be fun but I can

tell you in all honesty,' she said, eyeing the swimming
pool and the sun loungers, 'that if I don't move away
from this house, I'll be more than happy.'

'But you must! Don't let me stop you. The car's there,
you must take off any time you like and do *not* worry
about me.'

'We'll see. Right now I'm going to make us a nice pot
of tea. I wonder what time Lucia comes?'

'In good time to make lunch, according to Russ.'

Lucia arrived at eleven on the dot, as Anthea was
making the tea. It was only then that she learned
precisely what the couple's routine was. Between eleven
and two Lucia cleaned and made lunch; she was dropped
off and collected by her husband. Pedro worked as a
gardener at this villa and at several others. He also had a
'some time', meaning part-time, job in Los Cristianos.
During the evening, Lucia came back from six until
eight, unless she was instructed otherwise.

'Goodness, it sounds as if you both keep very busy!'
Anthea mused.

'But there is plenty of time, *señorita*! If you like me to
bring the food for you, you say so. There is a
supermercado only——'

'No, no, that's all right.' Anthea wasn't going to ignore
Aden's advice—or had it been an instruction?

'Please,' Lucia was saying, 'you will go outside with the
señora and I will bring your tea. And, *señorita*, you will
give me your washing——'

'Oh, I don't think so——'

'But yes! It is what I am paid for!'

'I see. Er, Mr Russell——' She got no farther. Lucia's
arms went up and she beamed.

'Señor Russell! He is such a gentleman, no? And so

bonito, so handsome. He is very good to me and Pedro. Even when he is not here and there is little work, we watch the house for him and he pays us. He is a good friend to you, too?'

He's no gentleman, Anthea wanted to say. She couldn't acknowledge him as a friend, either. 'He's my friend's nephew,' she said instead, gesturing in the direction of the veranda. She was safe, she'd dodged the question and Sybil was out of earshot. 'My friend is *señorita*, by the way, not *señora*.'

Lucia looked concerned suddenly. 'Yes, I forget. She . . .' There was a pause. 'The lady never marry? Not ever? She is not a—how do you say it—widower?'

'Widow. No, she never married.'

'But this is a shame! To have no husband and no children.'

Anthea wished she'd never got into this conversation. It was just like talking to her own family as far as the subject of marriage and children was concerned. Anthea's sisters, all three of them, were extremely good at producing children. Barbara had two, Janice and Alison had three apiece—and Janice had a fourth on the way.

She looked directly at the older girl. 'Not so, Lucia. Lots of women are very happy without children and without marriage, thank you. I'm one of them. It does *not* mean we're unhappy or unfulfilled.'

There was no answer, just a look of curiosity bordering on disbelief. Oh well, the Spanish—Canarians or whatever—were like that. Child mad. Lucia had to be forgiven; she came from a different society. At least times had changed in England, for the most part.

Anthea took her sunbathing very gently that first day. She would, she knew, turn a satisfactory golden-brown but only if she took it easy to begin with. Otherwise she would peel. Her skin was sensitive but it was, in fact, something she could not complain about, her complexion always having been blemish-free even when she was a teenager.

Sybil didn't move off the veranda. She was, she said, getting acclimatised. The two of them chatted from a distance of a few yards, Anthea getting up now and then to dive in to the pool. Late in the afternoon, after *siesta* when the shops re-opened, she set off for the supermarket in Aden's car, having been told by Lucia where the nearest one was.

The driving itself was fine, getting used to staying on the wrong side of the road needed concentration, especially when making a left-hand turn. But she coped and, having gained courage, went in to Los Cristianos after leaving the supermarket.

Everything was reported to Sybil later. Sybil had news, too—she'd had visitors while Anthea was out.

'A charming couple. Scottish, Mr and Mrs MacIntyre, they're from Edinburgh originally and they live in that villa over there,' she said, pointing. Since she and Anthea were in the dining-room at the back of the house, it didn't mean much. 'Anyway, guess what? Oh, I should explain that they came over because they thought Russ was here. They were full of compliments about him, said he was a charming man and so on. Actually, it seems he took their daughter out once or twice when she was visiting them. They're retired and live here all year round. I must say I agree with them in that it's good to be away from our winters at home. But where was I? Oh, yes! Guess what?'

Anthea was laughing at her. Something had excited her, she couldn't imagine what it might be. 'I have no idea and if you gave me twenty guesses, I'm sure I wouldn't be right.'

'They play whist.'

'Oh-ho!'

'Not just them, there are a few involved. A card school. There are some people who live in Playa de las Americas, apparently, who are very keen. I've been invited to go over to Mr and Mrs MacIntyre tomorrow afternoon for a game. They offered to come for me but I took the liberty of telling them you'd take me.'

'Of course I'll take you.'

'It's all very boring to you, darling, I know. An afternoon of cards, I mean, which is right and proper at your age. But it'll keep me quiet, won't it? I wonder why Russ didn't mention this?'

'He can't have known.' Anthea was delighted, not because she wanted Sybil to keep quiet, far from it, but because she was so obviously pleased. Perhaps, ironically, it was Sybil who had been bored? She asked.

'No, not bored. I've been sleeping so much, I haven't noticed time pass. In fact, had you not been doing the same, I'd have wondered about it. Since you have, it's obviously the change of air.'

It was true. Anthea had slept an abnormal amount since her arrival. 'That's what it is. I'll just be used to it when it will be time to go back. You'll be OK, having a whole month here. Lucky thing!'

'It's such a pity you'll have to go back.'

'You'll have Aden—Russ.'

'Even so, it would be better to have both of you.'

As it happened, Anthea woke on Saturday morning feeling positively energetic. She looked at her watch: quarter past eight. She'd slept for nine hours. So things were levelling off a little in the sleeping department. About time, too.

She wrote a note which she left in the kitchen and took off for the beach for a swim in the sea. So different from swimming in a pool, she couldn't decide which she preferred, actually. But how nice to have a choice!

She was by the pool in the villa during the afternoon, having duly delivered Sybil into the hands of Mr and Mrs MacIntyre, at which point she'd been given a large sherry which had gone straight to her head. Sherry always did that to her but it had been so difficult to refuse . . .

By three o'clock she was asleep in the full glare of the sun, oblivious to it and to everything else. When a shadow fell across her body, she was not aware of it, she was deeply asleep. Even when she was spoken to, she didn't wake. It was only when a hand touched her shoulder that she was jolted back to the here and now.

'Anthea?' There was a gentle shake. Her eyes sprang open and she gasped, momentarily alarmed and disorientated.

She gaped at the figure bending over here, shadowing her face now. Was she dreaming? No. He was touching her, his hand feeling cool against the heat of her skin, cool and—and by no means offensive. What was he doing here? Worse, why did she feel no disappointment on seeing him? 'Aden! What—why——'

'How, who, where and when.' He straightened up, grinning, his eyes moving inch by inch along her bikini-clad body. 'We-ll! Have I got a lot be grateful for!'

'To—to whom?'

'To the Fates,' he said. 'How kind of them to free me so I could come here early.'

CHAPTER SIX

EVERY instinct in Anthea made her want to reach for her wrap. But she didn't. It was too silly. For whatever reason, Aden was here, and she couldn't spend her time fully clothed for the rest of her holiday.

'I had the dickens of a job getting a flight, actually,' he was saying. He lowered himself on to a lounger, still eyeing her. I had to fly from Luton, couldn't get a flight from Heathrow. It's—Anthea, loath as I am to suggest this, I think you'd better cover up, you look as if you've had enough sun for today.'

She was about to tell him she knew exactly what she was doing, but she changed her mind and covered herself. She still wasn't over the shock of his turning up like this. 'What—how did you get from the airport?'

'By taxi.'

'Why didn't you let us know you were coming?'

Aden had already removed his jacket, now he was taking his shirt off. Anthea looked away, she didn't need to look to know what his body was like. She remembered it well, he was the hairy type, big and solid. 'We're not on the telephone here—or hadn't you noticed?'

'Of course I've noticed. You—you could have phoned Pedro and Lucia, or one of the neighbours. The MacIntyres——'

'How do you know about the MacIntyres? Have you met them?'

'Yes.' She explained about Sybil, her delight in her

discovery of the card school.

'Really? I didn't know about that.'

'And you've managed nicely to deflect my question,' she said. 'You chose not to warn us, didn't you?'

He smiled in answer. 'Why spoil what's turned out to be a very pleasant surprise for you?'

'Don't flatter yourself.' It was about the best she could manage. She *wasn't* disappointed he was here. It didn't make sense, but that's how it was. 'So what happened? How come you were able to get away, I thought you were involved in some big court case?'

'It was a case of case dismissed,' he grinned. 'You can't try someone who's dead, can you? We mortals can't, at any rate.'

'What are you talking about?'

'Haven't you seen the papers? No, I suppose not. If you had you'd have been expecting me. Half expecting me, at least.'

'I rarely read the papers.' Sybil did, but she hadn't since their arrival. As a matter of fact she'd mentioned only this morning that she was missing her *Telegraph*, and had asked Anthea to ask Pedro to bring one for her from now on. It would be yesterday's news, she said, by the time English papers reached the islands, but that didn't matter.

Aden shrugged. 'The man who was on trial committed suicide on Thursday night.'

Anthea was horrified. 'Your client?'

'No. I was prosecuting. Don't look so stricken, Angel Face, the man was as guilty as sin, an out-and-out villain. Nobody's going to shed tears over him.'

'What a callous thing to say! Somebody must have loved him, if only his mother. And how do you know he was guilty when the trial never finished? They can't have heard all the evidence——'

'You are an innocent, aren't you? More so than I thought. Do you always go around with your head buried in the sand? Why don't you keep up with the news, what's going on in this world?'

'I know enough about what's going on in this world—and I don't like it very much. The news is depressing, it's never good.'

'So you prefer to pretend it isn't happening.'

'No, I do not. I simply prefer not to wallow in mankind's miseries over my morning tea.'

Aden stood up, looking down at her. 'Go on, if you try harder you might turn this into an argument.'

'I don't want . . . I'm on holiday, I refuse to argue with you.'

He crouched down, catching hold of her chin and forcing her to look at him. 'Then we must make certain,' he said quietly, his green eyes lit with mischief, 'that we have fun in some other way.'

Anthea didn't know what to say, where to look. All she could do was lower her eyes. His words had been nothing short of suggestive.

'Blushing, Anthea? Why?'

'I'm not blushing! I'm—overheated. I'm going to have a swim. Kindly let go of me, Aden.'

He let go of her but he didn't let her off the hook. 'Overheated, eh? Too much sun, or what?'

She moved away from him, trying to calm herself inwardly. Then she turned and gave him her sweetest smile. 'You must have some unpacking to do. Are your cases inside?'

'In my bedroom. Why don't you come and help me?'

'Why don't you take a walk into the sea?'

'Aw, Anthea! What a killjoy you are. At least take that wrap-around thing off before you jump in the water, mm?'

She did. She took it off, folded it neatly and put it on her lounger, telling herself once more that she would have to get used to his eyeing her. The trouble was that her bikini, emerald green and silky, left little to the imagination. Not that she had felt self-conscious in it before, even on the beach when she'd been whistled at. It was just—just *him*, he had a way of looking at her which reminded her she was a woman, every curvaceous inch of her. She dived into the water. Aden had disappeared when she emerged.

A little later he reappeared, wearing tight white swim trunks and a pair of battered sandals he promptly kicked off. Anthea braced herself as he dived into the pool, convinced he'd pursue her, that she'd be in for a ducking at the very least. She didn't know whether to be relieved or disappointed when he kept his distance, swimming relaxedly but relentlessly, length after length.

She got out of the water after she'd counted twenty of them and sat by the poolside, wondering whether this show was for her benefit or whether he was as fit as he appeared to be. His body, she conceded, was magnificent. All animal. When he pulled himself on to the side of the pool, next to her, he wasn't even puffed.

'Enough for one day, it's been a long time since I last swam,'

'Then you must be as fit as a fiddle.'

He seemed surprised. 'Of course I am. There are other ways of taking exercise.'

In the face of her silence, he let it go. 'What time did

you say you'd collect Sybil?'

'At six. Maybe you'd like to go for her, give her a surprise?'

'Why don't we both go?'

'OK. Meantime, I'm going to have a nap.'

Aden caught hold of her arm as she got up, his eyes searching hers with no hint of amusement now. 'Anthea, you're not still avoiding me, are you?'

'No.'

'The truth?'

She smiled, a genuine smile. 'It's the truth. For what it's worth I've come to the conclusion you're not as bad as you make yourself out to be.'

He shook his head, tapped himself on the ear. 'I didn't think I'd got water in here!' Then he was pulling a face of such exaggerated puzzlement, she couldn't help laughing. 'I can't decide whether that was a compliment or not, madam! As bad as I make myself out to be? My God, this, when I've been trying so hard to be at my most charming with you?'

'Ha!' She straightened, put both hands on her hips and looked heavenward. 'I've heard everything now!'

She was asleep when Aden went to fetch Sybil. The first thing she knew, it was seven o'clock and there was the vague sound of voices coming from the living-room. When she opened her bedroom door she also became aware that something was cooking in the kitchen.

'Here she is.' Aden got up as she joined them. 'I didn't have the heart to wake you, you looked like Sleeping Beauty when I came for you.'

He'd been looking at her while she slept?

'Anthea?' Sybil looked at her curiously. 'You have no retort? How about: "Then it's as well you're no Prince

Charming"? I'd have expected at least something of the sort!'

She laughed. 'I missed my chance, didn't I? Must be because I've only just woken up.' It wasn't strictly true, some such remark had flitted through her mind.

'What you don't know,' Aden told his aunt, 'is that Anthea and I are going to be very nice to one another while we're here. Isn't that right, Anthea?'

'I—we can try. Did you have a nice afternoon, Sybil? A good game?'

'Delightful! Such nice people, the MacIntyres. Which reminds me, Aden, why didn't you tell me they were keen on whist?'

'My darling aunt, I didn't know. Why should I? I've only met them a couple of times. Actually, I met their daughter first, on the beach. A bit too flighty for my liking, as it turned out. She introduced me to her parents when we discovered they were my neighbours.'

'Well, you certainly impressed them, they were very complimentary about you.'

As if they'd just communicated telepathically, both Sybil and Aden paused and turned to look at Anthea.

She held up her hands. 'No, I will not be provoked. I will *not* say that there's no accounting for taste. I wouldn't be so rude!'

Sybil frowned, Aden's eyebrows went up, Anthea laughed. 'Anyway, are you over your shock, Sybil? I mean the shock of your nephew turning up?'

'I'm over it. Isn't it awful, though, about that man committing suicide?'

Aden wouldn't have it, not even from Sybil. 'Believe me, that man was *bad*. He would have spent many, many years behind bars, and he knew it. I've no doubt at all that that's why he did it.' Even more firmly he said, 'Furthermore, I don't want to hear another word about it. I'm on holiday, too.'

The two women exchanged looks. There would be not another word about it.

'If you were going to get me a drink, Aden, I'd like a Campari with lots of soda and lots of ice, please.'

'And you, Sybil?'

His aunt shook her head. 'No more for me, thank you. Dinner's at eight, Anthea. Lucia's slaving away in there.'

'Perhaps we'll go out to dinner tomorrow,' Aden suggested. 'So, ladies, tell me what you've been up to, where you've been.'

'Well, I've been as far as the MacIntyres, which is as far as I feel inclined to go.'

'And I've been to the supermarket and to the beach at Los Cristianos.' Anthea took the drink Aden handed her, grinning at the look on his face.

'My God! What an intrepid pair! The neighbours and the beach, yet! You'd better take it easy, girls, you'll be exhausting yourselves.'

Sybil knew what was coming, Anthea didn't. 'Now don't you dare start bullying, Russ. You might not be able to sit still all day but I find it no problem at all. However, Anthea is a different matter. She's been such a good girl, I know she wants to go off exploring the island but she wouldn't, she wouldn't leave me. Which is ridiculous, of course, but——'

Anthea denied that. 'It's neither ridiculous nor true. I needed to unwind, relax.'

'And have you?' Aden asked.

'Yes.' She raised her glass. 'Good health.'

'Then we'll start tomorrow.'

'Start what?'

'Our sightseeing. I shall be your chauffeur and guide.

It was no use, she couldn't deny the pleasure she felt. The idea of being driven around the island, of exploring, was very welcome.

'Good! That *is* good,' Sybil proclaimed. 'But count me out.'

'Let's play it by ear,' Aden suggested. 'We'll tell you where we're going, what we're going to do, and you'll say whether or not you want to come. All right?'

It was agreed.

The days that followed were exciting for Anthea. Not only did the weather continue to be glorious, except for a sudden shower late one afternoon, but she also had to admit she couldn't be in better company. Aden was like a different man. Or was he? How could she tell, how could she know, really? She had never given him a chance before, had never given herself a chance to discover he could be genuinely witty, that he could laugh easily, be both interesting and informative, could wax philosophical when he was in the mood. To her surprise, a very pleasant surprise, she found she enjoyed his company more and more as time passed. She found herself laughing a lot, found herself wondering whether she were different—whether they were both, simply, gripped by a holiday attitude, being carefree and adventurous as they were.

Tenerife was full of contrasts and Aden knew the island well. Sybil joined them only once on their outings. Apart from that they were alone, enjoying together all the sights worth seeing. Aden showed Anthea everything from the craggy, towering cliffs banking the dramatic seascape at Puerto de Santiago to the three thousand year old dragon tree at Icod, from the Esperanza Forest to the busy port of the capital, Santa Cruz. They spent a couple of hours wandering around the market there, with Anthea constantly expecting Aden's patience to run out as she moved from stall to stall.

It was when she was trying shoes on that she looked up to find him watching her intently. 'Are you bored, Aden?'

'Not at all.' He seemed a little offended. 'Far from it. Why should you think that?'

'Because I'm behaving like the typical tourist.' She laughed, glancing at the stallholder, an oversized lady who was hovering and fussing, darting away now and then to bring more and more shoes.

'You mean the typical woman,' he amended. 'That's fine with me. I'm enjoying myself, Anthea, I find your interest, your fascination with everything, very sweet.'

Sweet? She didn't know about that but she was fascinated by everything. This wasn't the first market she'd visited here but it was about the best yet. There was everything from leatherwear to jewellery, cameras, watches, perfume, hand-embroidered clothes which were so different from anything she could buy at home, inexpensive too, especially if one bartered.

The woman selling shoes turned to Aden, her arms outstretched as if in supplication, talking to him in rapid Spanish.

'What's wrong with her?' Anthea had already put two pairs of shoes aside, bargains too good to be missed. She was sitting on a wooden crate trying the shoes on, it wasn't the most comfortable of seats but that didn't worry her. 'Does she think I'm wasting her time?'

'No, no.' Aden was laughing. 'She's raving about your looks, your fair hair, your "eyes very blue", your slenderness.' He paused, lifting his eyebrows. 'Er—what she actually said was how very beautiful my wife is . . .'

Anthea glanced at the woman, wishing she could speak Spanish and put her right. 'Oh, well,' she laughed, 'we all make mistakes.'

'There's more——' Aden caught hold of her arms and pulled her to her feet. 'She said we made a "magnificent" couple, that we'd have very beautiful babies.' His clear green eyes were looking straight into hers and, much as she wanted to, she couldn't look away.

'And what did you say to that?'

He didn't answer for a moment. He let his hand slide up her bare arms, coming to rest lightly on her shoulders. On the periphery of her vision Anthea was aware of the woman; she was muttering to herself now, watching them. 'I'm afraid I lied,' Aden said quietly, his fingers tracing a line from her shoulders to her throat, then up towards her chin. He tilted it, holding her head still with his index finger. 'I told her we'd already had our first and that she was right, it was a beautiful baby.'

Anthea didn't know where to look, didn't know why she was so embarrassed by his little joke. She did, however, know very well why she was tingling where he had touched her. 'That was naughty, Aden.' She brushed his hands away. 'I'll—I must pay her. It's—it's time we got something to eat, I think.'

Aden excused himself, laughing at her discomfort, telling her he'd be back in a few minutes. Anthea settled her business with the stallholder and waited, feeling acutely self-conscious because the woman was still prattling away. She was relieved when Aden came back, carrying three packages wrapped in brown paper. Gifts, she assumed, for people at home. One of these days she would have to shop for gifts herself, she had at least to find something nice for Gail. Still, there was plenty of time for that. It could prove to be quite a headache.

The day she and Aden visited the Botanical Gardens, they were both snap-happy, their cameras clicking, again like typical tourists. Aden was more guilty of it than she, he kept making her pose against the colourful plants and trees.

'Aden,' she protested at length. 'What is all this? Would you mind telling me what it's all about?' He'd been taking her photo with his camera, not hers. 'What are you going to do with that lot when you've had them developed?'

'Look at them, of course. Now keep still and shut up.'

'But——'

'Anthea!'

She shut up, kept still while he clicked away. 'I'll give you any I don't want to keep,' he said when they were leaving. 'If there are any. You see,' he added, linking her arm under his, 'exotic and beautiful though everything is here, it's all pale in comparison to you. Without you as the focal point, anything I photographed would be boring.'

Anthea hooted at that. 'Flattery will get you nowhere, Mr Russell. It serves only to make me suspicious.'

Suddenly he was serious, very. Amid a crowd of people he pulled her into his arms, startling her. 'Suspicious?' he demanded. 'Why suspicious, Anthea? I can't believe you chose that word by chance.'

She hadn't. Beyond all the laughter, the fun, there was the irrepressible suspicion that he had ulterior motives

for all his kindness, his attention, his flattery. It was the
reason she was deliberately keeping her distance in spite
of their being together. It was the reason she removed his
hands whenever he touched her even in the most casual
way. She still didn't trust him wholly and—and she didn't
trust herself, either. Her awareness of him was acute; if
she dropped her guard things could very easily get out of
hand . . .

'Well?'

'I—please let go of me, Aden. Remember where we
are.'

'Where we are? So what? I believe you owe me an
apology and if it isn't forthcoming I shall punish you
right here, in broad daylight with dozens of people
looking on.'

She apologised, blinking when he threw back his head
and laughed. 'I see! Anything but that, eh? Anything but
being kissed. Poor Anthea! One of these days my
patience and your defences will run out, and then where
will you be?' He still had hold of her. He pulled her
closer, brought his face very near so that his mouth was
only inches from hers. 'No, *don't* look away, I'll answer
for you. You'll be in my arms, you'll be in my *bed!*'

'Aden——'

'Why the blush?' He shook her. 'Why look alarmed? Is
the prospect so awful? You know I want you, it's not
news to you. And the crazy thing is you want me, too. I
know it. But you're afraid. One of these days you'll tell me
why, of what.' He let go of her then, was content just to
take her hand as they headed for the car. 'You can relax,
Anthea. You have nothing to fear from me. As long as
I'm reading these "hands off" signals, I'll do just that. So
you can stop being suspicious. If you think I'm going to

pounce on you, you're wrong. I'm far too proud to seduce you into something you don't want, something you don't want with your mind, that is.'

His words made her think. She felt inwardly disturbed. was quiet almost to the point of silence during the next hour or so, until she had sorted it all out. Over lunch she kept looking at him, seeing him differently each time. She was learning about him, more and more his character was opening up to her.

Was this the real Aden Russell she was seeing now? She believed so. He was nothing like the man she had thought him to be, the man she'd been so angry with, so set against from the start. She had already developed a sneaking regard for him, something more than merely liking him, and today, just now, it had doubled. She had grown to respect him. He was honest, blunt, he said what he meant and he meant what he said. She liked that in a person.

He was right, she had nothing to fear from him. There were fears but they were in her own head, they had nothing to do with him personally. She had been wrong to feel suspicious of him. 'Aden.' She interrupted him in mid-sentence, having no idea what he'd just been saying. She wanted to apologise properly this time, it had suddenly become important to do so. 'I'm sorry—about what I said earlier. I mean it this time.'

He merely smiled, and covered her hand with his. 'I know. It's OK.

She smiled back, feeling light-hearted now, for some reason. It was a mood that continued for the rest of the day. It was only when she was in bed that night that she questioned it, that she realised Aden was having a strange effect on her.

She was different, here, now. How much was due to his influence? Was it the effect of Aden or was it merely that she was on holiday? She tried to tell herself it was only the latter, that she was happy because of her surroundings, that her spirits were high because of the sunshine and so on. But it didn't really ring true. It was him, him.

She didn't sleep too well that night. Or rather, sleep was a long time coming. The admission that she liked Aden Russell very much was disturbing. She didn't want to like him this much. Nor did she know how it had happened, really. It just had.

She had to be careful.

Warning bells were ringing, she had to be very careful indeed. While he'd told her in as many words that he would not take advantage of the attraction she felt for him, he certainly wouldn't refuse if she gave him the slightest encouragement.

CHAPTER SEVEN

THEY made the trip to the summit of Mount Teide the next day. Sybil didn't want to go, she said she'd been up several mountains in her time and could live without it. They didn't worry about leaving her while they went sightseeing; she had Lucia for company in the middle of the day or she was collected by the MacIntyres, where she was introduced to other people. Anthea and Aden were always back by six, in plenty of time for dinner. Anthea refused flatly to go out alone with Aden in the evening. She would not leave Sybil by herself in spite of her protests. Besides, being alone with him at night would be different from being alone with him during the day. She was too aware of him for her own liking; whether they were driving, swimming, walking, whatever, she was *aware* of him and she didn't want to invite trouble by putting herself in a situation, an atmosphere all set for romance.

And yet . . . and yet everything was romantic, Mount Teide, perhaps, most of all. It was also awe-inspiring, the view was absolutely magnificent, the air near its summit pure and rare. It was strange, feeling the heat of the sun while standing on snow-covered ground.

'I can't believe it.' Anthea turned to Aden, laughing after they got out of the cable car which took them virtually to the top of the mountain's highest peak. 'To think that down there people are sunbathing, yet I'm feeling chilly in spite of the sun. Oh, it's gorgeous, isn't it?

Must take advantage of this fresh air!'

He was smiling at her, slipping his arm around her shoulders and pulling her close. 'Cuddle up if you're cold. See? You wouldn't believe me when I told you to bring a heavy sweater.'

'Of course I believed you. I brought one, didn't I? And you will kindly stop that, Aden,' she said, backing away, 'I'm not *that* cold. Come on, let's walk, I want to see this view from as many angles as possible!'

They spent the whole morning on the mountain, talking, admiring, marvelling. For once it was Anthea who did most of the talking, she was waxing philosophical herself that day. It must have been the effect of the mountain. Whatever, she told Aden a great deal about herself, allowing herself to be encouraged, led by him, whenever she stopped. 'Tell me more,' he kept saying. And she did.

The inevitable happened when they were leaving the village of Garachico, a charming little port in a delightful setting. They'd seen everything there was to see, had wandered along the front, along the narrow streets, had poked their noses in the shops and visited the old castle, where they got snap-happy with their cameras again.

It was on the Saturday, a week after Aden's arrival and more than half way through Anthea's holiday. She settled in the passenger seat when they got back to the car, ready to head for home, a little breathless from the walk up the hill, laughing at something Aden had just said when suddenly his arm came around her shoulders.

'My God, you look so beautiful, laughing like that. Your eyes, they're vividly blue and——'

'Don't,' she said softly. She knew what was coming and she wanted his kiss almost desperately. It made her panicky. 'Don't spoil things, Aden. We—it's all so . . . so delicate.'

'Meaning you still don't trust me, that you're still wary of me. I'm—your opinion of me hasn't changed at all, has it? All this time we've spent together and you still think me a bastard.'

'No!' She groaned, aloud. 'Oh, Aden, it isn't that.' She thought she meant it. A second's further thought told her otherwise. 'Yes,' she said dully. 'I mean, I don't think any such thing but—it's hard to explain. Look, we're having a lot of fun, I just don't want to risk something going wrong, risk spoiling it.'

He was listening keenly, his eyes not leaving hers. When she'd finished talking he said, 'Now supposing you tell me what you really mean? What you've said doesn't make sense. What are you afraid of? *What?*'

In the face of her silence, very gently he went on, 'I want to ask you something. Please tell me now. What happened with your fiancé?'

That *was* it. He knew, somehow, that her wariness had something to do with that. She turned away. 'He—died.'

'*Died?* But—for heaven's sake, how old was he? You were only——'

'He was twenty. He was a medical student. I met him within days of moving to London to start my training. I'd wanted to leave home, to have a complete change of . . .' That wasn't relevant. She turned back to face Aden, finding herself able to tell him quite easily. That was odd, she wasn't emotional, she was very far from the heavy sadness she'd always felt when talking about Tony before. 'He ended up as a statistic. He killed himself on a motorbike. I'd never known anyone more *alive*. Then, quite suddenly, he was dead.'

Aden was silent for seconds. 'I'm sorry. I'm really very sorry, Anthea.'

'Thank you.'

There was another silence. He was watching her, neither of them moving. Then he reached for the ignition key and turned it, bringing the engine to life. 'And you're still in love with him.'

'No!' She was shocked. Still in love with him? That wasn't true. 'You're way off beam, I got over Tony's death, in time. It's five years ago, Aden.'

He didn't comment, he pushed the gear lever into first and drove off. Half an hour later they stopped for lunch and it was as if they had never had that conversation, those moments of awkwardness. They got back to the villa at a little after four, laughing when they spotted Sybil's note in the living-room.

They could hardly miss it. It was written in minuscule handwriting but it was on a huge sheet of paper which she had stuck on the door leading to the kitchen.

'Hello, darlings,' it read. 'Hope you've had fun. I'm in Playa de las Americas this afternoon—and will be all evening. I'm at the home of Mr & Mrs Stephen Baldwin (no relation to the old PM), for cards and dinner. I hope you have no need to contact me there, however. Do your own thing tonight, will you? Love, S.'

'Did you ever get the feeling you're not wanted?' Aden laughed, pulling the note from the door. 'Right! We'll go out. I'll pop out and talk to Lucia, tell her not to bother coming.'

'I——' There was no way Anthea could reasonably refuse. Lucia was long overdue a night off, Sybil would be cross if they stayed at home when they had no excuse to, and, most of all, she knew Aden would brook no argument. She could tell from the look on his face, he was virtually challenging her to protest. 'That—sounds lovely,' she said, bringing a smile to his lips.

'Off you go then.' He grinned, patted her on the behind. 'Go take your *siesta* then make yourself—no, you don't have to work at it, do you? You'll look beautiful anyway.'

Anthea escaped, needing to think. It was no use. She wanted to go out with him tonight, she wanted to be in his company all the time. Not once had it occurred to her to go off on her own this past week. How had he done it, how had he changed her attitude towards him? Had he made a conscious effort or had it just—just happened?

Their evening began perfectly and it continued like that. Everything went right from the very beginning, she emerged from her room knowing she looked her best, her hair was just as she liked it, well behaved, loose and curly to the top of her shoulders. Her shoulders were bare but for the shoestring straps on the bodice of her dress, which was the blue of her eyes and was her new favourite, knee-length, full-skirted and very feminine.

Aden didn't voice his approval when he saw her, he didn't need to. He merely looked her over and smiled. Anthea did the same. He was wearing a white jacket, was otherwise very casual with a pink, open-necked shirt and grey slacks. No words were exchanged until he handed her a drink, the Campari and soda she favoured.

'Thank you.' She took it, smiling, relaxed. 'I wonder what your colleagues would say if they saw you like this— a pink shirt?'

He chuckled. 'The same applies to your patients, they see only the young woman in the white overall. Mind you, a white overall does nothing to hide your figure, though I must say I prefer you in that dress.'

It was all so natural, their conversation, the teasing, her linking his arm as they walked to his car. The moon was full, the stars twinkling in clusters, the night still and velvety as they drove to the coast road and headed north.

They ate at a restaurant on the shore, an open air place which had enough customers to create the right atmosphere without their impinging, without Aden or Anthea noticing them. It was a seductive atmosphere, with the sound of the sea, the faintest breeze, the flowers around them in abundance, the candle on their table burning in its amber-coloured glass, the sweet night air all combining to make a magical evening. A troupe of musicians drifted in, their music preceding them softly. Unobtrusively they moved from table to table, were given glasses of wine, flowers, *pesetas* and applause. Anthea was enchanted by them, her attention shifting for the first time away from Aden.

'Hey,' he whispered, his hand reaching to cover hers. 'And there I was, thinking you only had eyes for me tonight.'

Slowly, knowing what she would see, she raised her eyes to his. All that was ordinarily striking about him seemed accentuated now, the shot of silver at his temples, the green clarity of his eyes . . . and in them she saw desire. Her gaze moved to his mouth, her wish, her need to be kissed by him suddenly overwhelming her. For seconds she became detached from everything, totally unaware of her surroundings, unaware of everything but Aden. She didn't even notice the fading music as the troupe walked away to the applause of the other diners.

'I think it's time we left,' Aden said quietly, and she nodded.

She was in his arms before they got in the car, before they even got near it. They'd walked barely ten yards from the entrance to the restaurant when he caught hold of her hand, pulling her easily towards him. 'Anthea . . .'

The first kiss was prolonged, hungry, it had been denied for too long and—and it wasn't enough. Anthea's arms slid inside his jacket, her need to touch him no longer blocked by her fears, her intellect. It was impossible to say how long they stood like that, Aden's mouth on hers, moving now and then to her throat, her closed eyes, back to her lips. She heard his words, spasmodic but linked, making perfect sense. On hearing them she knew they were her sentiments, too, but she knew that only as she heard them. 'I want you,' he told her, 'I've wanted you all along. You've been driving me crazy this past week, do you know that? Do you know how hard it's been for me to keep my hands off you? What I want to know is——'

They were interrupted. Four people called out as they emerged from the restaurant, walked past them in the direction of the car park.

Aden inclined his head, shrugged good-naturedly. 'They're right, did you hear that last remark? Do you speak French?'

'Quite well, actually, but I didn't hear the last remark.'

'Well,' he smiled, sliding his fingers into her hair, 'one of them suggested we head back to our hotel . . .'

They got in to the Spitfire. Nothing was said on the way home, there didn't seem to be anything to say. Anthea couldn't have explained her feelings if someone had paid her to try. They were jumbled. She wanted

Aden Russell as much as he wanted her but—something was stopping her. The spell had been broken. Reality was back, her capacity for reasoning working overtime now. In the darkness of the night she glanced at him, knowing there was going to be trouble. She had responded, encouraged him, and now she'd changed her mind. How could she explain, how could she explain it to him when she couldn't explain it to herself?

When they pulled up outside the villa, Aden switched off the engine and turned to her. He did not touch her, he didn't speak for several seconds. At length, quietly, he astonished her by telling her what she'd just been through.

'All right, Anthea, I know exactly how it is. You've lowered your safety curtain, put it firmly in place again, and I want to know why. Come on, let's get indoors and we'll talk it through.'

There was no sign of Sybil. Aden muttered something about her and went to check her room. He came back smiling. 'She's home, out for the count.' He switched on all the lamps in the living-room, sat in the chair set at right-angles to the one Anthea had chosen. A chair. For safety. He even knew why she'd done that.

'If you still think you're in some sort of danger, you're wrong. So if you'd be more comfortable on the sofa, you can move there with an easy mind.'

She looked at him. 'I—you're pretty smart, Aden. Maybe you can tell me why I switched off.'

'Maybe I can at that,' he said. 'Stop me if and when I go wrong.'

CHAPTER EIGHT

HE PAUSED briefly. 'I've worked at it, Anthea, I've worked at changing your opinion of me, and at trying to understand you. We've been together sixteen hours a day this past week, yet you've managed to keep your distance. I went along with your unspoken wishes because I could sense you didn't trust me. And you're still wary of me, you denied it today but you are.'

She looked at him. It was true, she had been wrong to deny it. It had nothing to do with him personally, not any more, it was just that he ... he was someone she was attracted to, someone she wanted. And she didn't want to want him. It made her feel as if she wasn't in control, of herself, her life. It made her vulnerable, open to being hurt.

'Say it,' he implored. 'Don't just sit there looking at me, tell me what's going through your mind.'

She couldn't, it would tell him how much she ... what? Cared. *Cared.* Quickly she got up, the very acknowledgement of the fact that she cared for him was more than enough to panic her. 'I've had second thoughts,' she muttered. 'I'm going to bed, there's really no need to analyse things. In fact, you've got a nerve if you think I owe you an explanation. Yes, I wanted you—out there, when we left the restaurant, but I changed my mind. It's a woman's privilege.'

'Hold it!' He caught hold of her wrist. 'What is this— attack is the best means of defence? That won't do, Anthea, it's not good enough. You're going to stop running away from me as of *now*. I'm tired of it; if you're not doing it physically, you're doing it emotionally.'

'What's the matter, Aden? Can't you take a refusal? Is it too much of a blow to your ego? Other women jump in to bed with you at the drop of a hat, I suppose——'

'Stop that.' He shook his head in disgust. 'I'm not talking about sex, and you know it. You've just admitted you wanted me tonight. You still do. Sit down.' He gave her no choice. When she made to walk away, his grasp tightened and he yanked her back into the chair. 'I'm trying to understand you, Anthea. I want to learn about you, to know you, not because I have ulterior motives but because I like you. Very much. Now why the barriers? Do you realise, all week you've been laughing with me, talking to me—yet you've told me nothing about yourself.'

'Don't be silly, I told you all about my family, my childhood, my teens——'

'And that's where you stopped. Your story ended with your leaving home to start your training. Only today did you tell me about your fiancé—and I had to drag it out of you. Since you're convinced you're no longer in love with him, not hankering after him, perhaps you can tell me what's holding you back as far as I'm concerned?'

'Involvement,' she said dully. Why not tell him? 'I'm afraid of getting emotionally involved again. I never have—not since Tony.'

Aden was looking at her as if she'd said something stupid. 'Emotional involvement? Good grief, is that what's holding you back? Surely you don't think it's what *I* want? Involvement is hardly at the top of my agenda, you know!'

His words should have reassured her but they didn't. In effect he had told her tonight that he wanted her but there was no danger of his becoming involved. Perversely, it angered her. She couldn't even admire his honesty, she had a mental picture of herself making love with him and then of his shaking her hand afterwards, saying he'd see her around or some such thing.

'Let go of me, Aden, you're spoiling what I thought was a perfect evening.'

'There's that word again, you used it this afternoon when you gave me the *hands off* signals. For heaven's sake, we're friends, aren't we? Why should it spoil things if we end up in bed together? Why not simply enjoy it?'

She didn't understand herself. Why didn't she go ahead and take what she wanted? Why not, when he'd assured her there would be no involvement? The answer came immediately: because *she* would get emotionally involved, that's why. To some extent she already was. Somehow, she had begun to care for him. It had sneaked up on her in the space of one week. How, why, when, she didn't know. It just had. She had to put up more barriers, had to make it clear that there was no way she would have an affair with him, with or without involvement.

Calmly, she said, 'You told me to stop you when and if you went wrong. Well, you just did. I don't consider us friends, we're just two people who happen to be on holiday together, who happen to like sight-seeing, who happen to be physically attracted. Maybe it'll help if I do tell you something about the person I am today, what I want from life, the way I think. If you'll let go of my wrist, I'll do just that.'

He let go of her, his expression one of dubiousness mixed with puzzlement. 'I'm listening.'

Anthea took a deep breath and tried to convince herself she had told the truth and was going to remain truthful. 'I'm content and happy with my life just as it is.

I have a good job, plenty of spare time in which I come and go as I please. I have no one to answer to, I have total freedom in every sense, and that's the way it's going to continue.'

He waited when she'd finished, still looking bemused, as if he expected more. 'Me too, as it happens. All of that. And so? What's your point? What has this to do with anything?'

'Nothing at all.' She got up, he didn't stop her this time. 'I just wanted to put it on record. You asked, didn't you?'

'I've met some complex women in my time, Anthea, but you win first prize.'

She walked away. Let him sort it out for himself. As for her—she had some sorting out to do, too. She undressed slowly, automatically washing and brushing her teeth before she climbed in to bed. Not that she'd sleep, she knew there was no chance of that. Her mind was churning, her emotions disturbed without a satisfactory explanation.

She was fully aware of the reason she feared involvement. It was too risky. She had loved her fiancé to distraction and it had taken a long time to get over his death. But she had got over her loss.

Or had she, in fact?

Oh, she was no longer in love with him but—but what about the after-effects? Wasn't her attitude today unhealthy, her fears almost phobic? Hadn't Gail told her a hundred times that she couldn't go through life in an emotional cocoon? She tried to, she made a deliberate effort to. Someday, some time, Gail had said, someone was going to penetrate it.

Someone had.

Of all the people in the world, it had to be Aden

Russell, a man with whom there would be no chance of—
of what? *What* was she thinking? Why was her mind
even working like this? Why, suddenly did she know she
had not been truthful when saying she was content and
happy with her life just as it was? Even before leaving for
Tenerife she had known a discontent, a discontent *he* had
created in her. She had called it many names—anger,
irritation, indignation. But there had been, there was,
more to it.

'Oh, God!' She sat bolt upright in bed, switched the
lamp on and put her hands to her temples. 'No! Don't let
it be that. Please don't let me be falling in love with him.
Not him. If you have to make it happen, let it not be
him!'

It was hours before she slept, fitfully, restlessly, but the
morning brought her a certain peace. She knew what she
had to do. It was Sunday, she would be leaving on
Tuesday. Two and a half days and she would be away
from him—away from the influence he was having on
her. Away from the disturbance. In the cold light of
morning she told herself she wasn't falling in love with
him—that there was, however, the danger of it. So the
answer was quite simple. She would avoid him as much
as possible. And when she was obliged to be in his
company, she would keep very firmly in place that
detachment he had complained about. What had he
called it, her safety curtain?

She had showered and dressed by eight-thirty. It didn't
surprise her that Aden was already up and out, taking a
swim. He pulled himself out of the water when he spotted
her. 'Good morning, Anthea. You're bright and early
today, I take it you slept well?'

She didn't answer that. 'Good morning.'

There was low laughter. 'You didn't sleep well.

Neither did I. So—where are we going today? I think we've virtually covered the island, unless you'd like to take another trip up the mountain?'

'I—thought I'd get to the supermarket early, there's quite a few things we need and it's closed this afternoon. It's—it's Sunday,' she added needlessly, feeling nervous. He was looking at her as if he didn't believe a word she'd said. 'You don't mind if I take the car, do you?'

'Now why should I? The keys are in the ignition but if you'll hang on a few minutes, I'll come with you and help.'

'There's no need for that, thanks all the same.' She walked away. She heard him call after her, saying they'd go to the beach when she got back, but she pretended not to hear.

Sybil was around, chatting to Aden, when Anthea got back from the supermarket. He detached himself immediately and came to help her with the shopping bags. Once they were in the kitchen, she thanked him and suggested he go back to his aunt.

'I can manage now, thanks. Why don't you go back to Sybil and I'll join you when I've put everything away.'

'Yes, ma'am, anything you say, ma'am.' He was grinning, touching an invisible cap. 'I can see I'm of no more use to you.'

She couldn't help smiling. 'Aden, if you helped put the groceries away, I'd never be able to find anything and I'm cooking lunch today. Lucia doesn't come Sunday lunchtimes, remember?'

He didn't say anything this time, he just left. He was back fifteen minutes later. 'What are you doing now?'

'I'm peeling potatoes,' she said patiently. 'What does it look like?'

'It looks like you're peeling potatoes.' He grunted.

'And lunch is hours away. Sybil's nodded off, come out and talk to me when you've finished that. I'm lonely and I'm missing you.' He disappeared again and came back shortly after. 'Now what? No, don't tell me, you're tossing a salad. Anthea, you do realise it's barely eleven o'clock? That could have waited a couple of hours. You're missing the sun.'

'I'll be out when I can.'

There was a short silence. She turned to see he was still standing in the doorway, arms folded, watching her. 'I thought you'd gone.'

He laughed. 'So it's back to that, eh? You're avoiding me again.'

'Nonsense. I'm making——'

'Excuses. You've been avoiding my company all morning. Now stick that thing in the fridge and come outside, have a swim with me.'

'No, I——' Aden crossed the room in two strides, took the salad bowl and put it in the fridge. The next thing Anthea knew, she was swept off the floor and thrown over his shoulder. She gasped, it seemed a long, long way to the ground.

'Stop that! What the devil are you doing?'

'You're going to take a swim.'

'No! Aden, let go of me!'

'Oh, I will, I will I assure you.'

'For heaven's sake, I'm fully dressed. Put me *down*!' They were already crossing the veranda. Sybil was in her usual chair there, snoozing, oblivious to Anthea's dilemma, her shrieks. '*Aden*, don't you dare do this! If you'll just wait a——'

It was too late. They were at the edge of the pool, right on the edge and he'd shifted her so she was in his arms now, looking up at him, her eyes sparking with anger.

Would he or wouldn't he? She kept perfectly still, glaring at him. 'Aden,' she warned, 'if you drop me, I'll never forgive you, it would probably ruin my——'

'Would you rather be kissed?' he asked, grinning because he was in control and she was at his mercy. 'I'll settle for that as a compromise.'

'No!'

'Oh, all right——'

'*No!* I mean—I mean, if that's the alternative. But make it brief.'

He didn't make it brief, far from it. While he kissed her she tried to blot out the pleasure of it, tried to distract herself by thinking how ridiculous this was. She was glad Sybil was asleep, what would she think if she opened her eyes and saw Aden on the edge of the pool, holding Anthea over the water, kissing her . . . and kissing her. When he finally lifted his head he had the nerve to tell her it had been no fun at all. 'Most unsatisfactory! I think I'd prefer——'

'Bastard!' she hissed. 'If you've quite finished amusing yourself, I'd be obliged if you'd put me down!'

Aden looked hurt. 'Name calling, eh? In that case, I will put you down.'

He dropped her into the water.

Anthea surfaced with some difficulty. She was wearing a full cotton skirt and a blouse, the sandals she'd bought especially for this holiday—which were probably ruined now. Spluttering and gasping she struggled to get to the steps and pulled herself up while thinking frantically of revenge.

Revenge was quickly forgotten. Sybil chose that moment to wake up. She squinted against the light, shading her eyes, no doubt convinced they were betraying her as she saw Anthea, fully dressed, furious, looking like a drowned rat, emerging from the top of the pool steps.

Anthea took one look at Sybil's face, heard her 'Good heavens!' and literally collapsed with laughter. They all laughed, and the more Sybil asked what had happened, the more they laughed.

'Well, it was like this,' Aden said at length. 'I threatened to throw Anthea in the pool and she tried to talk me out of it by offering to give me a kiss instead.'

'A kiss?' Sybil was interested, very. 'And did she? Did I miss that?'

'No, she changed her mind at the last minute. So in she went.'

'It's all lies, Sybil!' Anthea stood there, dripping. 'I did kiss him but he still——' She broke off abruptly. Aden was suppressing a grin but his eyes were full of laughter. At her. She had walked nicely into his trap. She glared at him, gave a very unladylike snort and went inside to change.

Her headache started in the middle of lunch, which they had by the pool, on the patio. She didn't say anything about it, she excused herself for a moment, slipped in to her room and took a couple of tablets. Aden was just refilling her wine glass when she got back. 'That's enough, Aden, thanks.' She wouldn't drink any more, wine in the middle of the day didn't sit well with her at the best of times. If she combined too much of it with headache tablets it would knock her out.

'What have you got planned for this afternoon?' Sybil was asking, going on to tell them she was playing cards with the MacIntyres and another elderly lady who was staying in a hotel at Los Cristianos. 'It's someone I haven't met before but I'm sure we'll have an interesting time. It seems she lived in India for many years, so we have something in common.'

'We're going to the beach,' Aden said. 'Anthea's in the mood for relaxing today, doesn't want to go sightseeing.'

She didn't want to go to the beach, either. Her headache was getting worse, the tablets hadn't had time to help yet. Still, it would be wise to make the effort. If she didn't go to the beach, it would mean she and Aden would be alone at the villa for the afternoon. Lucia and Pedro wouldn't show up till the evening. 'Tomorrow I must do some shopping,' she put in. 'I want to buy some presents. I can't think what to get for my flat-mate, there's so much to choose from . . .' Her voice trailed off when she saw the look Aden was giving her.

'Would you like me to drive you into Puerto? You'll have more choice there.'

'I—we'll see.'

Sybil was doing it now, looking at her curiously. 'Is something wrong, Anthea?'

'Not at all!' she said cheerfully. She wasn't going to mention feeling unwell. If she did, Aden would insist they stayed at home. Inwardly she was cross, with herself mainly. What the heck was the matter with her? Why couldn't she trust herself? And that was the top and bottom of it. It wasn't Aden she didn't trust, so much as herself. She heaped more salad on to her plate. Perhaps the food would make the headache go away. She hadn't had any breakfast.

Aden ran Sybil to their neighbours. He found Anthea in the kitchen when he got back. There was no dishwasher in the villa and she was washing up. He picked up a tea towel and started drying things. 'It's looking a bit ominous out there, clouds are gathering. Of course they can clear up as quickly as they appear down here. The south of the island doesn't get much rain.'

It rained. It rained, and how! Before they'd finished in the kitchen, it was coming down in sheets.

'So much for our trip to the beach,' he said. 'The one day we decide to go there instead of using the car.'

Anthea turned to him, grinning. 'That, my dear Mr Russell, is called Sod's Law.'

He inclined his head and caught hold of her by her waist. 'How right you are. So we'll have to think of some indoor activity we can amuse ourselves with, mm?'

Knowing he was only teasing didn't help. Anthea wriggled out of his grasp. She was feeling decidedly unwell, queasy, now, and it was on the tip of her tongue to tell him she was going to bed. She stopped herself. Aden would put his own interpretation on that! Actually to go to bed was more than she dared do, he'd think she was playing games, that it was some kind of come-on regardless of anything she might say.

She settled for a game of Scrabble. It was Aden's suggestion—made when she came up with none of her own. They were half-way through the second game when he asked her what was wrong. 'You look pale, I mean you've gone pale behind your suntan. Are you all right?'

'I'm—not feeling too good.' She was feeling sick.

He looked concerned. 'Why didn't you say something? If you'd prefer, we can——'

'Excuse me.' Anthea had no choice but to interrupt. She bolted, heading rapidly for her bathroom. She only just made it. She pushed the door closed, locked it and sank on to her knees by the loo. She was terribly sick, over and over again. When it stopped, mercifully, she heard Aden calling to her from her bedroom.

'Anthea? Unlock the door. Let me in, for heaven's sake!'

There was nothing he could do, nothing anyone could

do. 'I'm all right. I'll be out in a minute.' She dragged herself to her feet, rinsed her mouth, brushed her teeth, splashed her face with cold water. Then she saw her reflection in the mirror. She looked like death warmed up. It was just how she felt, too, her legs were so weak they were almost giving way. She unlocked the door and made no protest when Aden's arms came around her.

'My God! What is it?'

'I—don't know. I feel awful, really awful . . .' She was close to fainting, her ears were ringing, the room was shifting. 'Must be—must be something I ate.'

'No, but don't worry about that now.' He took control. She let him, in fact she couldn't have stopped him if she'd wanted to. He steered her towards her bed, his arms firmly around her. She sat down and he eased her back gently, lifting her legs, taking her sandals off. Her sandals had dried in the sun and were, she'd been surprised to find, no worse for their drenching.

Already her eyes were closed, it was too effortful to keep them open. 'Aden, I feel so weak, I can't describe it. Sorry . . .'

'Easy, take it easy, my lovely, and don't apologise. I wish you'd said earlier you felt unwell.' He was speaking softly, undoing the buttons on her blouse. She didn't attempt to stop him, she couldn't. Not for the first time, he was telling her how it was, why she'd behaved as she had. 'You are extremely beautiful and extremely idiotic, Miss Norman. You were being brave, weren't you?' He was unfastening her bra now, supporting her body with one arm while he reached behind her with the other. 'For your own sake as well as for mine. Scared to death, aren't you? Of me, and of yourself . . .'

Every word was heard, every word penetrated, yet it seemed to Anthea as if they were coming from a distance, his voice was familiar and unfamiliar somehow. She was able to think, was fully aware she was being stripped to her panties, that she'd managed somehow to get food poisoning, that Aden was being astonishingly gentle even while he was admonishing her.

'. . . didn't want to be alone with me here, didn't want to take off for bed. That's it, isn't it? Don't bother answering. It's typical of you. You know, one of these days you're going to believe that my interest in you goes further than the physical.' His hand was on her forehead, it felt cool against her skin. 'You're abnormally hot, Anthea. Can you hear me?'

'Yes.' Every word, she'd missed nothing, she was aware of his hands, both resting gently against her cheeks. She was burning up.

'I don't like this, I'm going to call a doctor.'

'No.'

'You've got a raging temperature, Angel Face.'

With an effort she opened her eyes. 'It's nothing—a touch of food poisoning. Just leave me, please. A few more trips to the loo and it'll pass.'

He laughed at that. 'I love your choice of words! But it can't be food poisoning, we've all eaten the same thing. Even last night you and I had a similar meal. Now hush,' he added softly but firmly. 'I'm going out to ring Doctor Linares, I'll be back as fast as I can.'

'No. Aden . . .' It was no use, he'd gone. Anthea immediately drifted to sleep.

The blinds were closed when she opened her eyes but she could tell it was still light. Aden was by her bed, he wasn't doing anything, he was just sitting there, watching over her. 'What time is it?'

'Five-thirty. The good doctor wasn't at home. I left a message, he'll come as soon as he can.'

'There's really no need——' Her first mistake was in attempting to sit up. There was no nausea now but her head felt as if it were made of lead, so heavy it was impossible to lift it off the pillow. She groaned involuntarily, bringing Aden to her side. He took her hand in his and held it gently.

'Tell me how you're feeling.'

'I'm—there's no sickness, no dizziness. I just feel—*ill*.'

'Well, hold on, I can hear a car out there. Maybe it's the Doc.'

It wasn't. It was the MacIntyres bringing Sybil home. She came in to Anthea's room with Aden, distressed and sympathetic. 'Oh, darling, what's happened to you? I've been told there's a bug going round, I do hope you haven't picked it up! It's a sort of three day 'flu thing, they say. Poor dear! What can I do for you, what can I get you?'

'Sybil, you are the greatest.' Anthea had difficulty in moving but she could at least talk. 'You wouldn't tolerate any fussing and sympathy when you were ill, and it was far worse than this. All I want is to be left alone, I'll be fine when I've had a sleep. So shoo—both of you.'

They left, Aden reluctantly, Sybil willingly. 'Come on Russ, we must do as she asks. We'll see what the doctor has to say,' she added pointedly, for Anthea's benefit. 'And we'll act accordingly.'

CHAPTER NINE

ACTING accordingly, as it turned out, meant cancelling Anthea's ticket for her flight home. Travelling was out of the question, she couldn't even get out of bed. She did have the three-day 'flu—as people were calling it, including the doctor—but it felt like something else and it lasted almost a week.

On the Tuesday night, the day she should have been going home, she went through the crisis, her temperature raging in spite of the medication the doctor had given her. There was no avoiding it, she knew, and she knew also that once past the crisis, she would be on the mend. By the early hours of the morning, however, she knew nothing at all because she was quite delirious.

There were only impressions, half-formed thoughts which didn't make sense. A man was there but she didn't know who it was. He held her hand and talked to her reassuringly. He kept going away and coming back again, putting something moist on her forhead, putting his fingers against her wrist, telling her she'd be much better in the morning.

What morning? What day? Where was she, and who was this? Everything was so dim. It wasn't her father, so who—it was Tony! *Tony!* 'Oh, my darling!' She caught hold of his arm, struggled to get him in focus. 'You're here, you're *here*!'

'Of course I'm here.' He spoke softly. She could tell he was smiling from the sound of his voice.

'Don't leave me. Don't——'

'I'm not going anywhere. Take it easy now. Hey, there's no need for tears. I won't leave you, I promise.'

'No, not ever ... ever ...'

He teased her. He shouldn't have. It was too upsetting. 'Not ever? Is that what you'd like?'

'Don't say that!' she shouted. 'I love you, I couldn't bear it. Not again, not again!'

'Again, Anthea?'

'Please, Tony! Tony, don't go away again, *promise me*!'

He promised. He gathered her in to his arms and held her against him, letting her take strength from his strength, reassurance from his reassurance.

Anthea was alone when she woke up. Or so she thought. There was no feeling of illness now, just weakness. She and the sheets she lay between were soaked with perspiration. She recalled nothing of what had actually been said, thinking she'd dreamt it all. 'Aden?'

He was in an armchair in the corner of the room. His eyes came open at once, at once he was on his feet, as if following a vital summons. 'Anthea?' Then he was by her side, taking her hand, touching her head. 'Feeling better?'

'Much. I dreamt ... it was awful.'

'Did you darling? About what?'

She blinked at the endearment, forcing a smile. 'Hey, it's me, remember? The one who's extremely idiotic.'

He didn't smile in return. 'So it is. And what about this dream? Tell me about it.'

'It was just—I thought Tony was alive. My God, I—was I rambling?'

Aden smiled then. 'No more than usual. I'm going to

need a little co-operation now, I want to change your sheets, they're soaked. If you can just roll to one side, I'll——'

'It can wait. Lucia can do it.'

'Anthea, it's five o'clock in the morning. It can't wait. You feel clammy and cold and this is no time for modesty. It's too late for that.'

She groaned inwardly. He was right, he'd seen it all, as near as made no difference. She rolled to one side and it took all the strength she had, even with Aden's help. She wanted to ask him who'd taught him to do this, to change bedding with minimal disturbance of the patient. But she didn't have the breath to make the effort. It wasn't that important.

She was in bed for four days in all. On the fifth and sixth day she got up for part of the time, went back to bed and slept again. Aden had been in touch with the airline and had cancelled her ticket, he also spoke to Gail and warned her not to expect Anthea home yet, asking her to talk to Anthea's boss at the hospital.

Anthea was horrified at not being able to get back to work—but it was hardly her fault. She would be teased about it, about taking an extended holiday, she knew, but she would be believed when she explained she'd been genuinely ill.

She did not, in fact, get away from Tenerife until Boxing Day. Sybil and Aden had got together in the kitchen to make Christmas dinner. Anthea offered to help but was put firmly in her place—her place being out in the sunshine.

Getting a flight before she did was impossible, the ticket she did get was only by a stroke of luck, the result of a last-minute cancellation.

A stroke of luck? Sybil thought otherwise. She complained volubly when Anthea was packed and ready to leave for the airport. 'Of course I'm coming with you,' she said to Aden, 'I wouldn't dream of not seeing Anthea off. I am not happy about her travelling home alone, Russ.'

'Neither am I. I would have gone back with her but there was only one seat, Sybil darling. I had a hell of a job achieving that much, so don't you dare accuse me of——'

'I'm not accusing you of anything. I just wish Anthea had company. It's a long journey and she's not well.'

Anthea was shaking her head. 'Now listen, both of you. Firstly I'm perfectly recovered and secondly—why on earth should you want to go home, Aden? You've got another week's holiday here.'

'I can take it or leave it. I've had a rest.'

Not this past week, he hadn't. He'd been conscientiously attending to her needs, he'd been wonderfully kind to her. Guiltily, she wished Sybil weren't driving to the airport with them, she would have liked to have a little time alone with Aden, to thank him properly. She looked at him, closely and carefully, feeling a sudden pain at the thought of leaving him, a pain so swift and sharp she could not deny that leaving him was the best thing she could do.

'Your gallantry is noted and appreciated,' she said lightly, forcing herself to smile, to hide her feelings. 'But you couldn't win. If you'd escorted me home, it would have meant Sybil travelling back alone.'

'Oh!' It was Sybil who was taken aback now. 'But of course, you don't know, do you?'

'Know what?'

'That I'm not going home. I mean, not next week.'

'What? But why?'

'Because I like it here, silly. Russ's original suggestion that I spend three months here has—suffice it to say I'm staying on. After all, it's freezing in England. You didn't see the papers last week. Surrey—the whole of England—is covered in snow. It's a stinker. I'd be potty to go back, to leave all this lovely weather, and it isn't as if there's anything in particular to go back for. Of course I'll miss you,' she added hastily.

Anthea smiled. She would miss Sybil, too, but there was no denying the sense in her staying on. She'd been so well here, was walking almost sprightly these days.

They set off for the airport. It was a quiet drive, hardly anything was said until they reached the airport building. Anthea kept looking out of the car window, enjoying the last of the rugged views, remembering all she had seen and done with Aden. Determinedly she put on a cheerful act when he and Sybil said goodbye; the last thing she wanted was to do what she was on the brink of doing, bursting into tears. It was on the plane that she did that, embarrassing her fellow passengers, no doubt. It was too bad, she couldn't stop. She'd been holding back more emotion than she'd realised and this was a safety valve. A good cry might exorcise her unwanted feelings for Aden.

At least they had never got out of control. She consoled herself with that. The danger of falling in love with him was over. What did they say? Out of sight, out of mind. Well, she knew from her own experience that that wasn't true, but an absence of two months or more would certainly help. It was time enough in which to get over him, especially when she was so determined to do precisely that.

Within an hour of take-off Anthea was in control again, her usual self except that she still felt weak. A day at home would be nice. She would rest and get herself together, in fact she was actually looking forward to getting home now, though she wished Gail would be there. Gail wouldn't get back from Ireland until tomorrow.

It wasn't until the plane was circling Heathrow that she picked up again on that thought. Having done so she was forced to admit that the prospect of being at *home* wasn't particularly welcome. She tried to tell herself she was being affected by the idea of freezing weather, she could see the snow now, lying thickly on the surrounding fields, as the plane began its final descent. But is wasn't just the weather. Resentfully, illogically she blamed Aden for bringing excitement into her life, if only with anger in the early days. More recently he . . . well, he had disturbed her in so many ways, her needs, her thinking, her emotions. Now, even the thought of getting back to her routine, which used to be more then enough to keep her happy, depressed her.

It would pass, of course. It couldn't be wholly because of Aden. She had the post-holiday blues as well. Almost everyone suffered from those at some point in their lives. They would wear off.

She brightened. All she had to do was forget, Aden, Tenerife, all of it. Once she *was* back in the old routine, she'd soon be the girl she used to be.

CHAPTER TEN

'YOU'RE not the girl you used to be,' Gail said impatiently. 'You've been moping for days, and I wouldn't mind but you haven't even got the courage to admit what's ailing you.'

Anthea still didn't feel one hundred per cent fit. It didn't help that she wasn't sleeping properly. Thoughts of Aden had been keeping her awake. To put it simply, she missed him.

She missed him terribly.

Nothing was going as she'd anticipated. Life was dull, flat, and it had nothing whatever to do with the rotten weather. It didn't stop Gail from going out and having a good time. She was working the day shift at the moment, doing the rounds at parties in the evenings. The day after tomorrow was New Year's Eve and she had a party lined up for then, too.

'Why don't you talk about it?' she went on. 'Talk about it, Anthea, *tell* me about it for goodness' sake, it'll help.'

Anthea looked up from the sketch pad on which she was doodling. They were in the living-room, Gail was doing her face in preparation for a date with Paul Patterson. She had, apparently, been seeing a lot of him while Anthea had been away. It had surprised Anthea because Paul didn't seem to be her type. He had nothing to do with the medical world, he was a garage owner, a widower, childless. He was comfortably off and certainly pleasant enough but—not Gail's type somehow. There again—who knew what laws governed attractions between men and women?

'There's nothing to tell,' Anthea shrugged. 'Aden and I are friends, that's all there is to it.'

She flung the sketch pad to one side and reached for the phone. Gail's constant picking was far from helpful. Anthea had had enough of it. She was about to get herself a date for New Year's Eve. No problem there. If she stayed home alone on that particular night of the year, she would be crawling up the walls. New Year's Eve was special. She picked up the receiver and put it down again, deciding to warn Gail before she spoke to Gordon Langley, the registrar who Gail fancied, who'd asked her out once—and only once.

'Anthea, what are you supposed to be doing?'

'I was—am—about to ring our dishy registrar.'

'Gordon?'

'None other. I thought I'd better warn you first.'

Gail's reaction to that was laughter. 'I might be a nag, but I'm not one to harbour a grudge. Go ahead, and good luck to you.'

Anthea nodded. 'Fair enough. For the record, I'm not ringing out of the blue, sort of thing. He asked me out the day I got back to work, he came over to me in the canteen and asked me to a party on New Year's Eve. It isn't the one you're going to, he said it was ... somewhere in Berkshire, I think. Anyway, I said no thanks. I've just changed my mind. Of course he might have asked someone else meanwhile. My hard luck if he has.'

'If he has, he'll get out of it. It's just what you need. Aden Russell is undeniably gorgeous but he's not the only fish in the sea. Gordon is equally attractive, in a different way of course, and he's been longing to get his hands on you since the day he met you.'

'He won't be getting his hands on me. Gail, why do you have to reduce everything to that?'

'Because that's what makes the world go round, dear child.'

'I thought love made the world go round.'

'What's the difference?' Gail asked, seeming serious. The phone rang.

Unthinking, distracted by the conversation, by the realisation that she could no longer communicate with Gail, Anthea picked it up.

'Anthea? At last!'

Her hand tightened on the receiver. It was Aden. The line was as clear as a bell. He might have been sitting in the same room.

'I tried ringing you last night and the night before but there was no answer,' he went on. 'I was getting worried so I rang the hospital to make sure you'd checked in to work. I didn't ask for you because—are you still there?'

'I'm here, Aden,' She saw Gail's expression change, from a frown to a smile, a big, ridiculous smile. It was followed by the thumbs-up sign. It helped because there was no way Anthea was going to enthuse in front of Gail, and in any case she didn't want to. She wanted to be friendly but casual. 'I wouldn't have appreciated being called to the phone when I'm at work. So how's your holiday going, how's Sybil?'

There was a silence. She was beginning to think they'd been cut off when he spoke again. 'You've been out in the evenings, have you?'

'A couple of times. I'm sorry about that.' She was lying, she had been in bed early, had heard the phone ring and ignored it. It was just as well she hadn't answered, though, she might even have given herself away by showing how pleased she was by his calling. There was no danger of her doing that now, not with Gail listening. And watching. 'How's your holiday going, you didn't say? And how's Sybil?'

'Since you insist on changing the subject—all right. Everything's fine here. I—Anthea, are you OK?'

'Fully recovered, thanks. I'm fine.'

'That isn't what I meant. I—never mind. I'm in a call box, actually. I've been thinking I'd better get a phone installed at the villa, after all.'

'If you do that, you won't be in control any more.'

Aden's voice was decidedly stiff now. 'Control? And that's everything to you, isn't it?'

'What? All I meant was you might get disturbed when you don't want to be.'

Silence.

'Aden?'

Quietly he said, 'I don't think we're on the same wavelength right now, Anthea. I think you're talking about something else.'

She held the receiver away from her ear, looked at it and put it back. 'You're in a very odd mood!'

'I was thinking the same about you. You're not alone, are you? Who's with you?'

'No one. I mean, Gail. Only Gail.'

'Make your mind up.' The stiffness had turned to coldness. 'I'd better go, far be it from me to interrupt something.'

'*Aden!*' The word came out passionately before she had time to think about it. 'You're not interrupting anything. I—just wanted to thank you before you ring off. I didn't have a chance to say it properly at the airport. You were ...' Damn Gail, she was laughing silently, looking heavenward. '... were very kind,' she finished lamely.

Aden grunted and rang off abruptly, before she had even had time to send her love to Sybil.

'What was all that about?' Gail wanted to know. 'If

you could have seen your face when you realised it was
him!'

Anthea shot to her feet. 'Why the hell don't you mind
your own business?' She was shaking, frustrated and very
near to tears. She went to her room, locked the door and
flung herself on the bed.

The way she'd shouted at Gail didn't worry her in the
least. The entire conversation with Aden had been
wrong, wrong! Her attitude, the words she'd used—she'd
wanted to be different, not effervescent but at least warm
and friendly. What impression had he got? She dreaded
to think. He hadn't seemed to believe her when she'd said
it was only Gail who was with her.

When the front door closed, signifying Gail's depar-
ture, Anthea determinedly dragged herself off her bed
and forced herself to make the call to Gordon Langley.
She had to pull herself together, to get out, to get Aden
out, too—*out of her system*. On hearing his voice tonight
she had been forced to admit that which she had denied
to Gail and to herself. Over and over to herself. But there
was no more room for rationalising, no way of avoiding
the truth. She was not merely in danger of falling for
Aden Russell, she was already in love with him.

She felt as if she were trapped in a blind alley, not
knowing which way to go, without light, without hope. It
had to stop, she *had* to lift herself out of this. Almost
desperately she plunged into conversation with Gordon.
If he thought her change of attitude towards him
baffling, he didn't show it, he kept her talking for almost
an hour.

'Why wait till New Year's Eve?' he asked at one point.
'Why don't we get together tomorrow night? I'll be on
call but——'

'No.' Anthea said the word again, more softly this
time, putting a smile in her voice. 'I have a few things to

do.' It wasn't true. She had nothing to do but she would invent something, if only cleaning the flat. It was the night after tomorrow that she didn't want to be alone. Tomorrow she would cope.

If she could have been forewarned then what would happen, she'd have thought differently. She didn't cope the following evening, she made a complete and utter mess of things. Her first shock was when Aden turned up on her doorstep—or rather, when the buzzer went and he spoke to her through the intercom.

Stupidly, Anthea stared at it, unable to answer for seconds. It was turned ten o'clock, she had spent the evening cleaning the flat, had just had a bath and was ready for bed. Fortunately she did not look a wreck. Her hair was almost dry and she was wearing the new nightdress and negligee set Gail had given to her for Christmas. It was of the palest pink and it did things for her, she'd put it on simply to cheer herself up.

'Aden?' she said at length, when he kept repeating her name. 'It's you?'

'Of course it's me. Will you open up, please? It's freezing out here!'

'Yes—I—yes.' She pressed the button, wondering about his mood. It was difficult to judge. Was he amused, cross or what? More importantly, why was he here?

Waiting behind the front door, as if on guard, she became aware that her hands were trembling. She just had time to tell herself firmly to pull herself together before Aden knocked. Composing herself was not easy but she made a good job of it. She even managed to be smiling when she opened the door.

He was smiling, too. Their eyes met and held in the sudden silence as they looked at one another. It was she who broke the silence, almost stammering as her heart began to pound uncontrollably, her very happiness at seeing him almost taking her breath away. 'Well, this is a surprise. You didn't say you were coming home today.'

'You didn't ask. To say the least, you were preoccupied on the telephone last night.' He was wearing a heavy, navy blue overcoat which seemed to make him look even bigger, taller. His eyes moved swiftly over her, taking in the nightwear which could only be described as sexy.

Anthea walked into the living-room, aware of his eyes on her. She turned, casually and sincerely laughing off what he'd said. 'Don't be silly, I told you, it was only Gail, sitting there and listening to me.'

The intensity of his voice startled her. 'I'm glad to hear that. Anthea——' He caught hold of her and in one smooth movement she was in his arms, her body sliding against his with the minimum of encouragement from him. They kissed hungrily, passionately, as if they had been separated for years, as if the past few days had been as painful for him as they had been for her, which could not be possible. Beyond her closed eyes Anthea seemed almost to be standing outside herself and looking on, her thoughts thrown into chaos except for the one thought which overrode all the others. *Stop this*, it was saying. This isn't the way you planned to behave, this isn't the way ... planned? What time had she had to prepare herself for this? Why was he here?

The question was chased from her mind when his hands moved to her breasts, cupping them almost roughly, possessively, as though he could not prevent himself. Immediately she broke free of him, but gently, laughing a little, trying to think of something to say.

He beat her to it. 'I missed you, Anthea.'

She found her voice, she even managed to sound light. 'So you said. I'm ... flattered. Sit down, Aden, I'll get you a drink.'

He frowned, looking straight at her, trying to assess her thoughts, her mood. 'I'd appreciate that.' Then he reached for her again but she side-stepped him. Still, he caught hold of her hand and held it firmly. 'I have to talk to you, that's why I'm here.'

Anthea could hardly breathe. He looked so intense, she didn't know what to expect, she knew only what she would like to hear him say. The impossible again! Was she going mad? Even as the thought zipped through her mind, she gasped in horror. 'Something's wrong, isn't it? Not Sybil? Oh, Aden, you haven't come to tell me——'

'No, no.' He was almost laughing at her now, his expression softening, his eyes almost a caress and they moved slowly over her face. 'It isn't about Sybil. Sybil is fine. She sends her love, by the way, and she said——'

'Are you there, Anthea? Hello?' A third voice joined theirs, a male voice, coming from the front door of the flat. Blankly Anthea looked at Aden and asked if he hadn't closed the door.

'I can't have.' His eyes were boring into hers, all softness, all tenderness gone now. 'You're expecting company, obviously!'

'No, I——' There wasn't time for more, no time to make him believe her, no time even to try and identify the voice. Its host had just walked into the living-room— tall, blond, handsome, and looking very cheesed off. It was Gordon Langley.

'I've just come from the hospital. Just got away from there, I should say, and I saw your lights were on—oh, sorry!' He cast an apologetic look at Anthea and, to her amazement, his face then broke into a smile and he held out a hand to Aden. 'Well, what do you know? Aden Russell, no less! What are you doing here, you old bastard?'

'Gordon.' Aden's hand came forward automatically

but his voice was like steel and it was Anthea he was
looking at. 'Long time no see, Gordon. You might tell me
what you are doing here.' Aden was as shocked as
Anthea, she was in no doubt about that. The difference
was that her shock was coupled with horror. What would
he make of this?

'How—how did you get in the main door?' she asked
hesitantly, her eyes flitting from one man to the next.
They were both standing, both still wearing their coats.
She didn't know what to do, what to say.

'Someone was just coming out.' Gordon had no idea
what he'd walked into, no idea what he'd *done*. He was
smiling, slapping Aden on the back now while she looked
on in bewilderment. 'I moved to Guildford a few months
ago, old man. I was saying, I've just got away from work,
thought I'd pop in and have a drink with Anthea. I must
say it's a shocker seeing you here. Fancy you two
knowing each other!'

Aden turned to Anthea, his eyes cold as ice. 'And
fancy you two knowing each other.'

She held his gaze, feeling anger as she did so. She
would not apologise for knowing Gordon Langley. Why
should she? Yet . . . yet she had to disabuse Aden of the
conclusion he'd reached, a conclusion which was
unmistakable. 'We work at the same hospital,' she said
hastily. 'I—wasn't actually expecting Gordon. Perhaps
you'd confirm that?' she added, appealing to the blond
man.

'Well,' he said obligingly, 'not tonight, at any rate.'

Anthea's eyes closed briefly. It was getting worse.
With a gaiety which was nearly wild in its falseness she
said, 'Why are we all standing like this? Sit down, both of
you! I'll get us a drink and you can tell me how you two
know each other.'

Gordon got only half-way through his answer. 'We

were at Cambridge at the same time. You're looking at *two* Cambridge Blues, you lucky girl! I was——'

'I won't stay,' Aden cut in. Indeed he was already on his way out of the room. 'Nice seeing you, Gordon.'

'Hey, don't dash off——'

Anthea chased rapidly after Aden and caught up with him at the door. 'Aden! Aden, I——'

'You don't need to explain anything,' he snapped, flinging the door open.

She saw red at that. She was also appalled at herself for running after him, literally. 'You're damned right I don't. But for the record, I wasn't expecting *either* of you,' she added quietly but firmly.

He merely raised an eyebrow. 'Not tonight, at any rate. Makes a habit of it, does he?' Then he was looking at her again, at all of her, his eyes travelling the length of her body in the softly clinging nightwear. 'This is certainly a new image, Anthea. Or is it? I thought I knew you. I was wrong, evidently.'

'Aden——'

'Wrong in thinking you honest,' he went on scathingly, giving her no chance at all. 'You told me you feared involvement, what you really meant was that you're already involved!'

'*No!* I——'

'Save it. Goodnight, Anthea.'

He was gone—*gone*!

She closed the door after him, there was nothing else she could do. Gordon was calling from the other room, she didn't know what he was saying but her first instinct was to go in there and blast him, tell him to get out. When she was face to face with him, however, he looked stricken.

'Hell, what can I say, Anthea? I'm sorry, very sorry——'

He sounded it, he meant it. It took the wind out of her sails. Tiredly she flopped in to a chair. 'It—wasn't your fault.'

Gordon looked at her with nothing short of admiration. 'That's kind of you. You see, I saw your lights were on and I just thought I'd——' He broke off, groaning, looking genuinely upset. 'I was just about to leave when he stalked off. I didn't mean to chase him away.'

Anthea almost smiled. She almost cried too. Anger and despair were fighting for precedence. Her anger was directed not at Gordon but at Aden. How dared he think her dishonest? How dared he assume that she and Gordon ... No matter how it had looked, he should know her better than that! Instead he had jumped to the wrong conclusion. She felt sick.

'Anthea? I'm—I don't know what to say.'

She looked up at Gordon standing awkwardly in the middle of the room, not knowing whether he should go or stay. 'Believe it or not, Gordon, you did me a favour.' She had just come to that conclusion. Had Gordon not put in an appearance—anything might have happened.

'I don't believe it,' he said quietly. 'Look, I'll—I'd better go, I think. Er—is it still on, our date for tomorrow?'

It was on the tip of her tongue to say no, not tomorrow or any other day. Not with you or with anyone else. Ever again. But the anger was still eating at her. After all, she was a free agent, wasn't she? Regardless of anything else, why should Aden Russell treat her otherwise? He presumed too much—he always had. 'Of course,' she said instead. 'I'll be ready at eight, as arranged.'

CHAPTER ELEVEN

'WHERE are we going exactly? I thought you mentioned somewhere in Buckinghamshire . . .' Anthea was dressed in black and gold. Her dress was black velvet, cocktail length, edged at the cuffs and hem with narrow gold braid which was the exact shade of her high-heeled sandals. A party dress for a party.

She was glad she had made the effort because Gordon looked splendid in an immaculate, dark grey suit teamed with a white shirt and a very tasteful, silk tie. She looked him over carefully as they drove away from her flat, acknowledging his handsomeness. Why was it one could be so strongly attracted to one man and not to another? Did looks enter into such matters at all, in fact? She thought fleetingly of Tony; he hadn't been particularly good-looking, yet she had been attracted to him from the moment they met. It was with Tony that she had planned to spend the rest of her life. Oh, they had had such plans! They would both work after qualifying, before starting a family. Then Anthea would have given up her career for a few years and—and now she was wanting that sort of future, that sort of life, all over again. With another man. It was incredible how her thinking had changed, how her mind had begun——

'You're not listening.' Gordon glanced at her worriedly. 'Where are you, Anthea?'

'Sorry.'

'I was telling you where we're going, about the party.

It'll be a big affair, over a hundred people I should think. Our hosts are very wealthy and very charming. David and Avis Freeman, they're both in their early fifties, an attractive couple. He's a brain surgeon, she's a psychiatrist. You'll like them. I've known them some years, I first met them when I was working in Leeds, where they used to live. I—are you with me, Anthea?'

'Of course I am! I was listening to every word.' At least, she had heard every word. She forced herself to brighten, to respond, to talk. She was going to enjoy herself tonight, no matter what. Maybe she would get drunk. No. Too risky when Gordon Langley was her date. She would have to keep all her wits about her. Gordon had a reputation as a womaniser.

'It's none of my business, I know,' he said suddenly, 'but I'm going to tell you all the same. He's a womaniser, Anthea. Don't get too involved. Or does my advice come too late?' He glanced at her, nodded slowly. 'Yes, I suspect it does. You were thinking about him just now, weren't you?'

'What?' Anthea was staring at him. She had been about to say she had no idea what he was talking about, *who* he was talking about, but no sooner had the thought formed than she realised. He was talking about Aden.

'At least he used to be,' Gordon went on, 'when I knew him at Cambridge. Maybe he's changed but I doubt it.' Struck by a sudden thought, he added, 'Assuming he is still a bachelor?'

Anthea didn't pretend ignorance. 'Yes, Aden Russell is still a bachelor, No, he hasn't changed. It seems you knew him pretty well.'

'Pretty well. No more. Through playing rugby, that's all. The last time I saw him was a few years ago, I bumped into him in a restaurant in London, he was with the most stunning redhead whose face I can actually recall to this day. I find him a likeable bloke. Just the same, I'm warning you off.'

She took no offence, indeed the conversation struck her as comical. 'You're a fine one to talk, Gordon. You have a reputation as a womaniser yourself. As a matter of fact I was just thinking about that when you said the same thing about Aden.'

He looked shocked, shocked and pleased. 'I have?'

'Come off it! You're charming and you're clever in more ways than one,' she said bluntly. 'And you don't fool me for a minute. Half the student nurses at the hospital are in love with you—even some of the more mature ones fall victim.'

'You make me sound like a villain.'

'I suspect you are.'

He wasn't laughing, he glanced at her and in the light from the street lamps she could see the seriousness in his eyes. 'I must have one saving grace or you wouldn't have agreed to come out with me—finally.'

Anthea was feeling more relaxed by the minute. For all his faults, she found she genuinely liked him after all. 'You have. Far be it from me to feed your ego but you're damned good at your job, for one thing.'

'And for another?'

'For another, I needed company tonight and you were as good as any.'

'Why, thank you!'

She laughed, real laughter this time. Then, suddenly and inexplicably, she was close to tears. 'I'm really being unfair to you, you know. Whatever you are or are not, you're not my type.'

'What you're trying to say is that you don't fancy me.'

She was fighting against tears, thinking about her mascara ... thinking about Aden. 'I'm sorry,' she whispered, 'but I have to be honest. I'm using you, Gordon.'

'I know,' he spoke just as quietly. 'You're in love with Aden Russell, God help you.'

'Gordon, I don't——'

'You don't want to discuss that. You're in a mess and you think you'll sort yourself out. Well, maybe you will, with a little help from your friends. I'd like to be one of them, Anthea. Believe it or not, I am capable of having a platonic relationship with a woman.' He sighed, lifting the mood to a merriment which they both made an effort to maintain. 'Dammit!'

They were friends by the time they reached the big house where the party was being held. It had taken an hour and a half to get there and they had talked about all sorts of things, about anything and everything—except Aden Russell. He seemed determined to help as best he could, was attentive and cheerful and charming. He introduced her to their hosts and to several other guests. When they mingled among the crowd, drinking and chatting to people, they stayed together. Gordon didn't leave her side for a moment during the first two hours.

When at a little after eleven he took firmly hold of her elbow and bent close to her, she thought he was about to tell her a joke or something.

It was no joke. 'Don't look now,' he said hastily, quietly, 'but you're in for a shock. Life is very strange sometimes, Anthea. I hadn't seen the man for several years—and now I find myself in his company on two consecutive evenings.' When Anthea merely looked blankly at him, he added gently, 'It's Aden. He's here, he's over there by the fireplace, with the tall brunette in red.'

Anthea didn't look. She didn't dare. She could feel herself going pale. Her gratitude towards Gordon was incalculable as he kept talking, kept his eyes on hers, kept rambling. 'He's looking. I'm going to give him something to think about, OK?' And with that he brushed a kiss against her cheek, slipped his arm around her waist.

No sooner had Gordon straightened up than Aden was striding over to them, leaving the brunette chatting to an elderly man who seemed to have appeared from nowhere. Anthea saw it all, registered everything. There were several new faces in the room, it seemed that people were still arriving. And whoever the brunette was, she couldn't take her eyes off Aden in spite of her having other company. It was as though Aden's presence had heightened all Anthea's senses, she was aware, alert, but thanks to Gordon she had had a precious few seconds in which to prepare herself for this encounter.

'Good evening, Anthea. Small world, isn't it?' Aden's voice was smooth but his eyes told a different story. He was annoyed, and it angered her immediately. What had he got to be annoyed about?

Just what sort of game was he playing? Here he was, at a New Year's Eve party with a girl who was not only beautiful but obviously deeply enamoured with him, while only last night he was making love to her, Anthea. Or attempting to. He might have succeeded, too, had it not been for Gordon's interruption.

'Good evening to you, Aden. Yes, it is a small world.'

She looked straight at him, her own annoyance clear to see.

'All these years,' Gordon put in. 'And we meet again, two nights on the trot. Strange.'

'Strange,' Aden parroted. He was still looking at Anthea.

'Have you known the Freemans long?' Gordon went on. 'How did you meet them? Were they clients of yours?'

'I don't know them.' Aden almost snapped at the other man. 'That is, I didn't until tonight. My . . . my colleague is a friend of theirs, a family friend.' His eyes came back to Anthea's before he turned, gesturing towards the brunette by the fireplace. She was alone now, started walking towards them with a friendly smile on her face.

Anthea felt herself stiffen. Even before the introductions were made she knew who the woman was. It was Fiona Calveley, the person who had telephoned the night before Anthea and Sybil had flown to Tenerife, when they'd had to stay over at Aden's house because of the fog. Fiona Calveley, to whom he had been so warm on the telephone.

As Fiona joined them, Aden's arm went round her shoulders and the gesture spoke volumes to Anthea. She was more than a colleague to him. Much more. As the two women shook hands Anthea caught a whiff of Fiona's perfume. Her dress was stunning and obviously expensive, scarlet and studded around the neckline with sequins of the same colour. Yet it was simplicity itself, ankle length and fitting like a second skin. Her figure was superb. Aged around thirty—possibly a little more— she was the sort of woman who turned heads. Her hair was sleek and shining, her eyes hazel and large and . . .

tinged with sadness. Anthea found herself looking into them for longer than she needed, longer than she should have. She felt almost sympathetic in that moment. She, too, had fallen under Aden's spell. Was she, too, hoping for something he would never give to any woman? Did Aden know it, if this were the case? Probably not. If he suspected she had become emotionally involved, he would drop Fiona Calveley like a hot brick. Except that she worked in the same chambers . . .

Fiona's laughter was enchanting. Anthea could almost feel Gordon's interest in her, though he was doing his best to keep his attention on Anthea. 'The music seems to have got louder, doesn't it? I was saying what a good party it is. Are you enjoying it?'

'Very much.' It was all Anthea could manage. The vibrations criss-crossing between the four of them were almost tangible. At least it seemed that way to her. She glanced at Gordon, willing him to come to her rescue.

He did. He made small talk with the other couple for several minutes, talking about mutual acquaintances. For Fiona's sake he mentioned Cambridge and rugby again, explaining how he knew Aden, and between him and Fiona there was a lot of 'Oh-ing' and 'Ah-ing' and 'What a coincidence!'

Aden said next to nothing. Anthea didn't know how long she could stand it, this horrible pretence she was putting on. Her smile felt as if it had frozen on her face, she envied Fiona's naturalness, her spontaneity.

'Why don't we dance?' Aden said suddenly. He was talking to Anthea, taking hold of her arm in that forceful, assertive way which annoyed her now more than it ever had in the past. 'And let these two get better acquainted?

You don't mind, do you?' He glanced, smiling, from Fiona to Gordon.

Gordon glanced at Anthea but she wasn't able to give him any sort of signal. Her face seemed immobile, her voice had deserted her. All she wanted was to get away—from this company, this party, this house . . . and this woman.

'Not in the least!' It was Fiona who spoke, seemingly happy. She linked her arm through Gordon's and flashed her eyes at him. 'Why don't we all dance?'

Which was precisely what happened. All four of them moved into the other room, where the music was louder and where the centre of the floor was crammed with couples dancing. Anthea began to feel light-headed, it was too hot in here and it had been a long time since she'd eaten. In yet another room a beautiful buffet had been laid out but she hadn't had a chance to tackle it yet.

She shook her arm free of Aden's grip with a suddenness which took both of them by surprise. 'I—if you don't mind, I think I'd rather get something to eat.'

He looked down at her, his eyes green and clear and speaking plainly of his feelings. 'I do mind. I'm going to give you the benefit of the doubt about Gordon Langley—provided your explanation is satisfactory. You *owe* me an explanation and you'll damned well get on with it. Now!'

'I owe you——' She got no further. Several people had turned at the harshness of Aden's voice and he swept her into the dancing now, his arm around her in a grip she knew from experience she would not escape. She fell into step with him because she had no choice, lowering her voice to a hiss. 'I owe *you* an explanation? For all your faults I'd never have thought you a hypocrite, but that's just what you are!'

'Hypocrite? What the hell are you talking about?' His arm closed so tightly around her, she could hardly breathe.

'Take it easy, will you? You're going to break my back!'

'I'd like to break your neck! What the hell are you doing with the likes of Gordon Langley? Unless he's changed drastically over the years, he'll be sleeping with—for God's sake, Anthea, he's a womaniser, a past master!'

Her laugh was curt, harsh, she spoke without thinking. 'Funny, he said the same thing about you.'

'Never mind that! I said—but I don't need to ask, do I? Not after last night's little scenario.'

'There was nothing in that. He just——'

'He just happened to drop in. So you said. Well, that's not good enough, Anthea. I am not satisfied with that!'

'And I am not on trial!' she countered. 'Remember that.'

He ignored it, mimicking her, 'He just happened to drop in. And you just happened to be dressed in pink candyfloss and all ready for bed, sweet-smelling and——'

'Stop it! How dare you? *Hypocrite*. That's what I mean.' Anthea jerked her head in Fiona's direction. 'Your accusations to me and now—*this*. Her!'

'Her? She . . .' He shook his head, he stopped dancing and looked at her as if she were crazy. 'Fiona's just a friend, you know that. We work in the same——'

'The same chambers. Well, Gordon and I work in the same hospital. So what does that prove?'

'Listen to me.' Aden caught hold of her shoulders and shook her. People turned to look at them but neither of them noticed. Anthea was sizzling with anger. She could not believe his nerve in talking to her like this. If she hadn't known better she might have thought him jealous. It was hardly likely. The only thing that ailed *him* was a bruised ego. He thought she was giving to Gordon something she had denied him. Well, let him think what he liked! 'I've heard enough, Aden, more than enough! Get away from me and stay away, *permanently*. You make me sick with your——'

'Aden?' Fiona had joined them, her face ashen. Anthea stared at her, totally at a loss. Quickly her eyes sought Gordon. He must have said something out of place. Dear Lord, he hadn't made a pass at her, had he?

He hadn't. It was obvious from the way he pursued her, caught up with her. 'What is it?' he was asking. 'Fiona, what is it? Did I stand on your foot or something?'

Fiona smiled weakly at his attempted joke but her eyes were almost desperate as she turned back to Aden. 'Aden, I want to leave—now. Right now.'

For split seconds Aden said nothing, he just looked at her. Then he took hold of her arm in that proprietary way of his, glancing briefly at Anthea and Gordon as he led Fiona away. 'Excuse us, Fiona and I have to talk.'

Neither Anthea nor Gordon knew where they went, what was wrong. They stood, looking after them as they left the room. It was Gordon who spoke first. 'I wonder what gives?'

'I—I've no idea.' Anthea was shaken to the core. The evening had caught up with her and she was almost dizzy with it, with anger, frustration, jealousy, curiosity. 'I thought you'd made a pass at her.'

Gordon's smile came quickly, it was an attractive smile which made his eyes crinkle at the corners. 'You do me an injustice. Grant me a little tact and finesse, Anthea. I'm forty years old, not sixteen.'

She smiled in return. An ironic smile. He was right. He was older, as was Aden, and older men, sophisticated men, did not make inappropriate or clumsy passes at women.

'Anthea?' Gordon spoke quietly, his face close to hers so he would be heard above the music. 'What's going on exactly? I mean what have I stumbled across? Is this the old eternal triangle bit? Is Aden in love with Fiona? Is she in love with him? If so, how do you fit in? I mean last night, why was he——'

'Don't ask,' she said, her voice equally soft, almost a sigh. 'Because I don't really know the answer to any of your questions.'

Gordon nodded, endearing himself to her by accepting and leaving it at that. 'Shall we get something to eat?'

'I think I'd like to go home, Gordon.'

'We can't do that, lovely. They haven't rung in the New Year yet.'

What he meant was that it would be rude to leave so soon, to leave before midnight. They got something to eat instead.

Midnight struck before they had finished eating. They and lots of other people abandoned their food and everyone gathered in the drawing room, a huge room filled with antiques which, had Anthea owned them, she would have put away for safety's sake.

Silence fell. A grandfather clock was chiming in the hall. Then it was midnight and a New Year had begun.

People were cheering and kissing, linking hands ready
for the inevitable old song . . . and she had never felt
more miserable in her life. Amid the crowd she spotted
Aden and Fiona, kissing and being kissed, they were in a
group of people some of whose faces had become familiar
during the course of the evening. So they hadn't left.
Whatever had upset Fiona had been talked about. She
seemed fine now. She was laughing, saying something to
Aden as she turned her face up for another kiss.

Gordon and Anthea left soon afterwards. They sought
out their host and hostess and thanked them for a
marvellous time. They did not make any effort to say
goodnight to Aden and Fiona. Nor did their paths cross.
Anthea slipped into the room where the coats had been
put, took Gordon's hand gratefully and let him lead her
to his car. Nothing was said for the first half hour of their
journey.

'I'm sorry,' she said at length, when eventually she
remembered her manners. 'I wasn't good company
tonight, Gordon. You'd have been better picking a name
out of your little black book.'

He roared with laughter. 'Do you mind? Your opinion
of me gets worse by the minute!'

'On the contrary.' She smiled, reached out a hand and
touched him briefly on the cheek. 'Eyes front! Don't let
this go to your head, this is just a gesture of . . . gratitude.'

'To hell with gratitude,' he muttered. 'I've been
interested in you since the first time I saw you—and don't
you dare jump to the obvious conclusions!'

When they reached her flat, Gordon surprised her by
accepting her offer of coffee. They both knew she was
suggesting no more than that. The place was in darkness.
It was almost three in the morning and she, they both,

assumed that Gail was still out partying. They were wrong. No sooner had Anthea put the kettle on than Gail appeared in the kitchen, looking bleary-eyed and shattered.

'Hello, you two. Good party?'

Gordon laughed. 'Looks like yours was. Happy New Year, Gail!'

'Happy New Year.' She muttered the words, sinking on to a kitchen chair. 'I'll have coffee too, please. Happy New Year, Anthea.'

'Happy—oh, dear.' It was only then that Anthea took a good look at her flat-mate. She wasn't merely bleary-eyed, she had been crying. 'You and Paul had a fight?'

'Paul and I had a fight. And then some. But let's leave it at that, shall we?'

Nothing else was said on the subject. The three of them transferred to the comfort of the sitting-room and drank several cups of coffee. Maybe that was a mistake. An hour later they all had a new spurt of life, were all wide awake. Anthea didn't mind, there was so much going through her head, she knew she wouldn't sleep. In spite of the hour. It was she who suggested they had something stronger to drink and both Gordon and Gail agreed at once.

'Don't mind if I do,' Gordon said. 'I can walk home from here.'

It was only then that Anthea realised fully what an unsuccessful evening this must have been for Gordon. She had begun by telling him she was using him, he had helped her through the encounter with Aden and Fiona—and he hadn't had a drop to drink except for the single glass of champagne he'd accepted at midnight. He wouldn't, couldn't, drink and drive.

Anthea opened a bottle of Scotch, poured three generous measures into glasses and left the bottle near Gordon. 'Help yourself, you deserve it.'

'Thanks, but no thanks.' He seemed amused. 'You two might have reason for drowning your sorrows, I haven't. Although . . .' He broke off, laughing at himself. 'I have to say this is an odd way to end an evening, here I am with two gorgeous women and neither of them is going to show the slightest interest in anything other than my riveting conversation.'

Anthea laughed, Gail did not. Anthea looked at her. It was as if she hadn't heard. She was looking down at the floor, was miles away. There was something different about her. This wasn't like her, not to have an answer ready, not to flirt with a man whom only weeks ago she had fancied like mad.

So that was it!

Whether Paul Patterson was Gail's 'type' or not, he had got to her somehow. They had fought, she'd said. And it had upset her far more than she was willing to show.

Anthea touched her shoulder, her eyes full of understanding as she spoke, softly and with just the right amount of sympathy. 'And a Happy New Year to you, too.'

It provoked a grin, a response. 'Yeah. Why don't I put some music on?'

'I don't know,' Gordon teased. 'Why don't you?'

It was ten minutes to five when he left. He went home on foot, letting himself out of the front entrance of the building quietly, by no means drunk but having had more than the legal quota. He would walk back for his car some time tomorrow.

Anthea and Gail went to their rooms without saying anything. There would be time enough to talk tomorrow. She would be able to talk to Gail now, at last. She was different. And she was needed. They needed each other, as they had in the early days. Needed to cry on one another's shoulders.

At the back of the building, in the comfort of his Rolls Royce, Aden Russell finally saw the lights go off in Anthea's flat. It was five minutes to five and he had been waiting for almost two hours, immobile in the blackness of the car park . . . in a corner. The BMW with the label saying 'Doctor' on the windscreen was still there, just fifty yards away from his own vehicle. There was no mistaking it was the right car, he had watched it drive away from the house in Buckinghamshire hours ago.

Several hours ago.

Aden waited five minutes more, he had to be certain. Nobody came near the BMW.

His face set in a mask of fury, he put the gear lever into drive and let the big car glide away. Homeward. To an empty house and what was left of the night.

Another sleepless night.

CHAPTER TWELVE

'PAUL asked me to marry him last week.'

Anthea's mouth fell open. '*What?* You—why didn't you tell me?' She and Gail were sitting at the kitchen table, drinking tea. It was almost two in the afternoon, New Year's Day, and they had been up for an hour. They hadn't eaten anything, hadn't moved, hadn't even started talking until now.

There was no recrimination in Gail's voice, just a sigh. 'I've been unable to talk to you. You've been— preoccupied. You've been thinking about Aden to the exclusion of anything else. I tried to get you to talk about him, to unburden yourself, but you've been like a clam.'

'That's because I thought you thought it a laughable situation.'

'*Laughable?* You don't really think I'm that hard, do you? Oh, Anthea, you should know me better than that. What *is* the score with you two? I know how you feel— but what about Aden?'

Anthea was quiet for a moment. 'Aden feels nothing for me—nothing except a physical attraction. Yes, laughable,' she repeated bitterly. 'And I'm the laughing-stock. I feel foolish. *He's* made a fool of me. The only consolation I have is that he doesn't know it, doesn't know I'm in love with him.'

'But what——'

'No.' Anthea held up a hand. 'You first. Tell me about you and Paul.'

There was a shrug. 'Not much to tell. Honestly, I

146

haven't known him that long, as you're aware. I like him very much but—well, his proposal took me by storm. I said no, instantly. He asked me to think seriously, carefully, about it. He painted a pretty picture of what our lives could be like together, how much easier things could be for me. I explained to him as best I could that I'm scared, that marriage to Sean had been a bitter experience, that it was something I wouldn't rush into again.'

'And?'

'And last night he gave me an ultimatum. He said we marry or we finish, don't see each other again.'

'So he's in love with you.'

'For his sins.' Gail smiled faintly.

'I take it you said no.'

'Of course I did. He was as good as his warning, he said we're finished. I told him he was being unfair, he should give me time, but he said he couldn't stand it, that he was in love with me and it had to be all or nothing.'

'I know the feeling,' Anthea said quietly. All or nothing. All was always too much to hope for, wasn't it? She reached across the table and covered Gail's hand with her own. 'I'm sorry for both of you. You want different things. It's going to be easier for you than it is for him. You're not in love with him.'

Gail frowned, shook her head. 'I—actually, I'm not sure about that.'

'That in itself should confirm it.'

'Since when did you become an authority?'

'Since now. Since I've admitted I'm in love with Aden. Admitted it to myself, I mean. If a miracle happened and he asked me to marry him, I'd say yes without even thinking about it. Two months ago, you'd never have thought you'd hear me say that, would you? I've already thought about it, I've dreamed about it . . .' The last words were added quietly because it was difficult to admit, even to Gail. 'See what a fool I've turned into?'

Neither of them smiled. 'So you've got over your fears,' Gail said. It was a statement, not a question.

'Love transcended them.' Anthea tried to be flippant, and failed. It was the truth. She had been thinking about the dream she'd had when she was delirious in Tenerife, the dream about Tony. For a few months after his death she had been haunted by such dreams, had dreamt he was alive but he was going to leave her. Yet she had experienced nothing like that for several years since, so why then, in Tenerife? Why, when it was Aden rather than Tony who was paramount in her thoughts?

The answer was that she had actually been in love with Aden then, at that point, though she hadn't realised it consciously. Or rather she had fought it, repressed it, because it had frightened her. The dream about Tony had been symbolic of that fear.

Yes, she knew the answers, she had thought it all through, had come to understand herself very well. Tony was gone, he would always have a special place in her heart . . . as a memory. A happy memory. He was in the past.

Aden was in the present. And she loved him. Loved him, loved him, loved him. The dream had been her mind's way of sorting everything out, putting things into perspective. Despite her delirium, or perhaps because of it, her subconscious mind had got its message over to her, though it had taken some time for her to decipher that message consciously. It was very clear now. She looked at Gail, sighing. 'I resisted loving Aden. Because of my experience with Tony I was scared to love again. To love and lose. Well, I did overcome my fears, I loved again . . . and lost.'

'You're sure there's no—I mean, how can you be sure of his feelings?'

Anthea laughed at that. 'Aden has no feelings. He's selfish, deceitful, egotistical, he wants——'

Gail was brought up to date in the minutest detail. Anthea told her everything—but everything. When she had finished, Gail said, 'He's got a nerve!'

'Quite. He was seducing me one night, out with Fiona the next. When I saw him with her at the party I knew then that any sneaking, stupid hopes I'd had were blown. Why hadn't he asked *me* to the party? Because Fiona is one of his stable of women, that's why, and it was her *turn*. Well, at least I'm getting generous in my old age because I actually feel sorry for Fiona. She and Aden are lovers, I'm in no doubt whatever about that. She's in even more deeply than I, poor girl. She looked haunted last night. Haunted. I've decided that her strange little outburst was jealousy. She affected not to mind Aden's whisking me off to dance—but she minded. She couldn't stand it.'

There was a silence. The two looked at one another.

'What now?' It came from Gail.

Anthea stood up and visibly squared her shoulders. 'I do what I did in the past. I get over it. I've already been through the crying times. I'll not shed another tear over that man. I shall pick myself up and dust myself off.'

And start all over again, Gail added silently. She watched her friend as she headed for the bathroom. She was uneasy. She didn't like the look in Anthea's eyes.

But Anthea was as good as her word. She cried no more. As the days passed she threw herself into her work with what seemed like a renewed vigour. She was tense, she was nervy and work helped. Every time the phone went at home, she jumped. Over and over again she cursed herself for hoping yet again, *praying*, even, that she would lift the receiver and hear Aden's voice.

Would she never learn?

During the following two weeks she went out with Gordon Langley as often as they could manage. Why he was being so kind to her, she could not imagine. She asked him finally.

'Because someone was kind to me once, in similar circumstances, when I needed a friend.'

'Are you going to tell me?' They were in a pub just outside Guildford, sitting by a roaring fire, sipping drinks. Gordon took his time about answering, and when he did he was positive but brief, very brief. 'Yes and no. You can take my word for it or not, as you choose, but I was faithful to my wife. I loved her and I wanted nothing and no one else. She was unfaithful—like every other day, she was unfaithful. It was a long time before I found out.'

They fell silent. Anthea was stunned. She believed him. Not only that, she was learning daily how odd life was, how full of surprises people were. How complex. How vulnerable.

Oh, how very vulnerable!

It was the following afternoon that Gordon came looking for her in the hospital. She was in the gym, working with a young man who had broken both his legs in a fall from a ladder.

'May I have a word, Anthea?' Gordon jerked his head in the direction of the doorway. She excused herself to her patient and wordlessly followed Gordon out into the corridor.

'What is it?'

He fished in the pocket of his white overall and waved a small piece of paper at her. 'I've just been given a message. It seems I had a phone call from a Mr Aden Russell. He asked that I ring him back.'

Anthea tried to look blank but her insides were curling. 'So why are you telling me? I mean, what has it to do with me?'

He shoved the paper back in his pocket. 'Look, I'm busy. I'm going to ring back but—just tell me what you want me to say when he mentions your name. Which he will. Don't be obtuse, Anthea, he has no other reason for ringing me.'

She was squaring her shoulders again. 'Then tell him to mind his own bloody business!' She went back into the gym.

For the entire afternoon her mind was crammed with questions, questions and that awful, persistent hope which would not wholly fade away. What was Aden up to? Why ring Gordon if he wanted to know something about her? Was he still interested in her? If so, why not ring her himself? Or was it just a social call? Did he want to see Gordon for old times' sake or something?

It wasn't until eight that evening that she had a chance to question Gordon, when they met in the pub they had been in the previous night.

'Well?' It was the first word out of her mouth as he joined her. She had already been there ten minutes, sitting by the fire, staring into it.

Gordon grinned. 'And a cheerful greeting to you, too.'

'Sorry. Hello, Gordon. What did he want?'

'He wanted to know, and I quote, *precisely* what my relationship with you is.'

Anthea gaped at him. She didn't know whether she wanted to throw a fit of fury or whether she wanted to laugh. 'God, what a cheek!'

'My sentiments entirely.' Gordon was only just lowering himself into a chair.

'So what did you say?'

He blinked at that. 'Exactly what you suggested I say. I told him to mind his own bloody business!'

Anthea's mouth formed into a soundless shape. Oh. Gordon had taken her at her word and she was disappointed beyond speech.

So that was that.

'Anything interesting?'

Anthea looked up as Gail walked into the kitchen. Saturday had rolled around. Again. Next weekend she, Anthea, would be away. She had three consecutive days off and she was going home. It wasn't the most delightful prospect but it would be a change. It was time she saw her family, time they saw her. 'It's a letter from Sybil.'

'I gathered that. Who else would be writing to you with an envelope marked "Tenerife"?' Gail helped herself from the teapot.

'She says they're going to install the phone at the villa in a couple of days. It's probably in by now, she wrote this days ago.'

'Fascinating.'

Anthea grunted. 'I can tell you've just fallen out of bed. And why are you up so early?'

'Because I'm on duty again at seven tonight and I've got a lot to do today. Thrilling stuff, like washing and ironing and shopping.'

'Thrilling.' They lapsed into silence and Anthea finished reading the letter from Sybil. That was how she would spend her next hour—answering it. Sybil was as entertaining in her written word as she was in her speech.

Amusing and informative. She was not bored, she said, far from it. She was enjoying herself and might even stay on till spring had well and truly arrived in England. Why not? Why not, indeed?

'Do you want to shower first?' she asked Gail.

'Do you mind? You were up first.'

'No. I'm going to have a very lazy morning, answer this letter and whatnot.'

'Are you seeing Gordon tonight?'

'Not tonight. I'm giving him time off.'

Gail frowned. 'I don't like to think of you being here on your own all evening.'

'I'm not a child,' Anthea said crisply. 'I can look after myself. In any case I'm on call this weekend.'

'You know what I mean.'

Anthea apologised at once. 'I'm sorry. Of course I know. But it's all right. It gets easier every day. Time does heal, you know.'

'You're sure?'

Anthea nodded. As Gail went to the bathroom, Anthea reflected on what she had just said. It was true. The hurt was beginning to fade. She thought about Aden just as much as ever—but it was hurting a little less to do so. Whether it had to, simply had to, because with every passing day she realised she had no choice but to go on, to try to behave normally, she didn't know. It was hard to differentiate between one's capacity for self-deceit and one's instinct for self-preservation. Whatever, she felt a little more confident now.

But her confidence was shattered only twenty minutes later. When the phone rang, she picked it up and it was only as she was doing so that she felt that awful surge of hope that it might be Aden. Hitherto she had hoped at the first sound of the phone ringing, had run to the phone instead of walking. That was progress, wasn't it?

'Anthea?'

'Yes, speaking. Who is this?' She glanced at the receiver, shook it a little. It was a female voice, familiar but not yet placed. The line was crackling quite badly. 'Hello?'

'Yes, yes, I'm here. Now what's going on? What on *earth* is going on?'

'Sybil! Sybil? Is it you?'

'Of course it's me. I've been trying to ring Russ and eventually his housekeeper answered. She said he left for Singapore on Thursday evening and he'll be away at least a week, possibly two. An old client has landed himself in some sort of mess out there and Russ—but never mind all that. Anthea, I'm at a *complete loss* to understand. Surely there's been some ghastly mistake?'

Sybil wasn't the only one who was at a loss. 'Mistake? What mistake? What are you talking about?' Anthea's stomach tightened. 'What's happened, Sybil?'

'You mean you haven't seen it? Oh, my dear, I'm sorry! You'd better sit down if you're not already doing so——'

'Sybil, please! Has something happened?'

'You obviously haven't seen today's *Telegraph*. I mean yesterday's *Telegraph*.'

Taking her friend's advice, Anthea sat down, lifting the phone on to her lap. 'You know I rarely look at a newspaper. Has there been an accident?' It couldn't be Aden, it couldn't be. If there had been something in the paper about his being involved in an accident, he wouldn't have flown to Singapore, would he? 'Please tell me, Sybil. Just say it.'

'Russell has got engaged to Fiona Calveley. The

announcement is there in black and white, in yesterday's
paper.'

The following minutes were unreal. Anthea was aware
of Sybil using words she had never used before with a
force which was equally uncharacteristic. She was
ranting. Every word was heard by Anthea but she
couldn't comment because she couldn't believe it.
Mistake? Yes, it *had* to be a mistake!

Yet it was there, Sybil said, in black and white.

Fiona Calveley. *Engagement*.

'Anthea? Anthea! Are you there?'

'I'm . . . I'm here.'

'Can you throw some light on this? He's never said a
word to me, it's hit me like a thunderbolt! I mean, I
thought——'

'It's—it's surprised me somewhat, too.'

There was a sudden silence, Anthea began to think
they'd been cut off. 'Sybil, are you still there?'

Her voice was quite different now, quiet and calm and
sad. 'Yes, darling. I'm—sorry, Anthea. It must have been
the most sickening shock. I'm very sorry. I don't know
what else to say.'

That made two of them. Anthea was stuck for words,
her head was reeling, her heart was hammering and she
felt close to fainting. Hardly anything else was said
before she and Sybil hung up. What was there to say?

'Anthea?' Gail emerged, wearing jeans and a thick
pullover. She found her flat-mate staring into space,
unblinking. In three strides she crossed the room and
caught hold of her, shook her. 'Anthea? Anthea! What is
it? What's happened? You look as if you've seen a ghost!'

The younger girl's eyes changed direction, focused on
Gail's face. But it was seconds before she could speak.

'Russ—Aden's—it can't be real. Not marriage, not for him!'

'What? You're not making sense. What's happened, for goodness' sake?'

'I just had a phone call. From Sybil. It was in the paper. Yesterday's paper. An announcement of Aden's engagement to Fiona Calveley . . .'

Gail stared at her. 'I don't believe it! I——' She didn't finish the sentence. She left Anthea where she sat and dashed out of the flat. Anthea didn't know where she'd gone, how long she was gone. The next thing she was aware of was Gail coming back in to the room with a newpaper. It was quite crumpled. She flung it on the floor and knelt over it, muttering to herself. '. . . never read the *Telegraph* but I knew Bob Hoskins would have a copy . . . Here's the section on . . . oh, my God, it's true! *An Engagement is announced* . . .'

Then the paper was under Anthea's nose and she saw it for herself. The formal announcement. In black and white. Actually seeing it was as much a shock as hearing of it had been. The floodgates burst, a whole new torrent of tears welled up and poured down her face. And she had thought there were no more, had thought she was getting over Aden Russell. She started sobbing and she sobbed until Gail thought she would never stop.

'Anthea. Oh, Anthea . . .' It was there in her voice, too, that heavy sadness she had heard in Sybil's voice. As if Anthea were bereaved.

All over again.

CHAPTER THIRTEEN

GOING to Bromsgrove, going home, had been a mistake. She could hear the buzz of conversation, the occasional squeal of a child, as she lay on the bed in the guest room, the room she had once shared with her sister Alison, the sister next to her in age. The curtains were drawn against the afternoon light, which was fading anyway, and her brain seemed to be beating a tattoo inside her head.

It wasn't that her family was getting on her nerves, something odd had happened in that respect. They seemed to know what was wrong with her, not only that there *was* something wrong, but what it was. They were all being very sweet to her, particularly sweet to her. On first seeing her, her parents had remarked that there was something wrong and had asked if they could help. She had told them no, there was nothing wrong. Perhaps she should admit the truth, even though she didn't need to.

But they couldn't help. No one could.

They were downstairs right now, all of them, her parents, her sisters Barbara, Janice and Alison, their respective husbands and the eight children between them. Anthea had been unable to stand it, had escaped upstairs after the ritual of the Sunday roast. It was wrong of her because they had all gathered under one roof especially to be with her. They were probably all talking about her now. But she had needed an hour, just an hour's solitude, so she had said she had a headache. Now, she really did have a headache. Her mind was spinning like a top, flashing pictures at her, pictures which would never become reality.

Something odd had happened to her, too. On previous visits she had seen her family so very differently. None of her sisters worked and she had thought them slave-like to their men, had been irritated with them for being so unambitious. And now she actually envied them what they had.

The children, when they were all together, had driven her mad in the past with their constant questions and need for attention, whereas now she had found a resource of patience she hadn't known she possessed. She was seeing them for what they were, they were her sisters' children, her nephews and nieces, little individuals, people who loved her.

Her parents used to have a depressing effect on her, too, with their bland acceptance of an unchanging life, an almost unvarying routine. And in the past they had put pressure on her, all of them, with questions such as 'When are you going to settle down, Anthea?' 'Do you intend to stick at that job for ever?' 'There was a time when you intended to marry . . .' 'You're not getting any younger, you know, and when it comes to having your first child, you should think about . . .'

She used to be almost desperate to get away, to get back to her own, uncluttered, unfettered life, the one she had tailored to suit her. But now . . . this time . . . she saw things differently. They were content, all of them. Oh, there were normal family differences, an occasional bark one at another, but they were *content*. There were four families downstairs, four family units. Four families making a big, whole one. Since leaving to start her training, Anthea had been the black sheep. She still was. She was different. She always would be because she really did want more to her life than her sisters had . . .

yet she wanted what they had, too, now. That and more. More and that. There could be several layers to her life; as it was there was only one. Her job was her only real satisfaction in her existence. If Aden were to marry her instead of Fiona Calveley, all her longings would ... there was no point in thinking like that.

No point. But she couldn't seem to stop herself no matter how she tried. Every time she closed her eyes she saw the pictures again. Her sister Janice sitting on the settee downstairs—seven months pregnant with her fourth child. Her *fourth*, yet on her face there was a look of contentment which bordered on the mystical; she was experiencing some deep, inner contentment, as if she had some special knowledge, some precious secret, no one else knew of.

She couldn't wait to get away from them—all of them. But her reasons were different now. Very different. With every minute she was here, they were showing her what she was missing.

She didn't need to be reminded any more.

Only recently had she realised that she'd wanted it all along, had merely repressed it during the years since Tony's death. Shoved it right to the back in the filing cabinet of her mind. But it was there, always had been. All it had taken was the right man to open the right drawer.

'Anthea?' At the sound of her father's voice, she sighed. She had known one of them would come to check on her, sooner or later. She hadn't expected it to be her father. He walked over to the bed, took hold of her hand and asked if she was feeling any better.

Richard Norman was sixty years old, his bushy hair had long since gone grey and his face had become more handsome with age, in spite of the lines on it. Maybe because of them. There was wisdom and understanding there now. Had there always been?

Two solitary tears escaped from the corners of Anthea's eyes and she nodded, her voice a whisper. 'I'm OK, Dad.'

'Who is he?' he asked quietly. 'What happened?'

There was no preamble, no need for that. No point, not any longer. 'A barrister. Nearly twelve years older than me. He's just got engaged to someone else. Last week.'

Richard Norman said nothing. There was nothing he could say. 'Come downstairs, your mum's making tea.'

'Give me five minutes,' Anthea said wearily. 'And—tell them. You can tell them what's what. Better coming from you than me.'

She went downstairs five minutes later. Not a word was said, not a single look of sympathy came her way.

She had never loved her family more than she did right then.

The train pulled away from the station at lunchtime on Monday, bang on time, and Anthea stood by the window with a feeling of heaviness. Her mother had bought a platform ticket and was standing there, waving as the train chugged away. When she was out of sight, Anthea moved away from the window and found a seat.

It was time to go back to Guildford. There was no escape, there or at home, in Bromsgrove. Geography made no difference. Gail would be at work, the flat would be empty. It would be silent and still and it would mock her. Silent and still, like the rest of her life. There was no . . . no *foundation* to it any more.

Someone tried to chat her up on the train, a young man several years her junior. Inwardly she smiled at his attempt, outwardly she cut him off with single syllable replies to his opening gambits. Firmly but not unkindly. She wasn't feeling unkind. Not towards anyone. Even Aden. Especially Aden. She really and genuinely hoped he would be happy with Fiona. That was how much she loved the man.

The flat wasn't silent when she got in, the telephone was ringing. Unthinking, she made a bee-line for it, registering only that the place was nice and warm. It was freezing outside. It was also getting foggy. She grabbed at the phone without switching a light on, though the flat was in near-darkness. It was early February and the days were still very short. She squinted at her watch as she spoke.

'Anthea? How're you doing? When did you get back?'

'Two seconds ago. Hello, Gordon.' She sank on to a chair, grateful for the sound of his voice. 'How are things with you?'

He laughed. 'I asked first.'

In other words, stop beating about the bush. 'All right,' she said levelly. 'I'm taking it a day at a time.' He, too, had been stunned at the announcement of Aden's engagement. Stunned, and then he'd gone on to say, only half-jokingly, that he'd been thinking of ringing Fiona himself, to ask her out ... Gordon Langley was incorrigible. But he was very likeable.

'Would you like to come out for dinner tonight?'

'No, I don't think so, thanks.'

He sighed. 'You should. You owe it to me.'

'What does that mean?'

'It means I've been stood up and I'm without female company for the evening.'

'You're hopeless.' But she was laughing, thinking about it. It would be better than sitting alone in here all evening. Of course it would, but she had a few jobs to do and in any case, she had to get used to it. Had to get used to this loneliness she hadn't known before Aden.

'Does that mean yes?'

'It means no. It means I realise what you're trying to do and I know you're being kind, putting the onus on me. I'm not falling for it, though. It's appreciated, don't misunderstand me, but you can't play babysitter for ever.'

'Actually, you're wrong,' he said, and he sounded serious enough. 'I really have been stood up. Some crazy woman who doesn't realise what she'll be missing.'

'Gordon——'

'And I'm in need of company.'

Anthea gave in, gave up. 'OK, we'll compromise. You can come here for dinner—which will consist of whatever happens to be in the cupboard. I honestly don't feel like going out but I'll chat to you while I'm doing my ironing.'

'Ironing? Oh, Anthea!'

'Shall we say eight o'clock?'

'I'm sorry I asked,' he muttered, and hung up.

Anthea put the phone down, grinning to herself. She put the lights on and headed for the kitchen and some coffee. There was a note from Gail propped against the kettle: 'Welcome back. Will be home around midnight with a man called Jack. Yes, it's a new one! He's nothing to look at but he makes me laugh. He's picking me up at the hospital when I finish my shift. See you. Love, Gail.'

Anthea dropped the paper into the rubbish bin. Her grin had extended to a smile. 'A new one!' How like Gail! Was she to be envied? Was she really content with *her* life, or was she kidding herself, as Anthea had been kidding herself for years? She checked the cupboards and the fridge, found plenty of food and several bottles of wine. Good for Gail. Gordon would be well fed tonight. She glanced at her watch again; if she got a move on she would be able to clear her ironing and the other little chores before he arrived.

He arrived on the dot of eight. She had learned that about him long since, he was punctual. He was a lot more, too. He was genuine, his charm was real, he was kind and he was thoughtful. What a pity that's as far as it went, for her. She knew full well it was different for him and it bothered her a little. In a way she was being unfair because if things carried on the way they were, there was a possibility of Gordon becoming emotionally involved with her. Never, not once, had he made a pass at her. She was constantly expecting him to, but he did not. She couldn't quite work that out.

'Good evening, lovely lady.' As she opened the door, he bowed.

She laughed at him. 'Poor dear, you look frozen! Come in.'

'It's a filthy night, foggy as hell. I walked round, thought it would be safer.' He thrust a bottle of red wine and a box of chocolates at her.

'Gordon, you shouldn't keep doing this . . .' He never came empty handed, he always brought some little thing with him when he came to the flat.

'Nonsense.' He followed her into the living-room, his eyes on the curves of her bottom in the tight jeans she was wearing. Anthea caught his surveillance, as she turned, and she ignored it.

'Help yourself to a drink, I have to check things in the kitchen.'

'It smells good, whatever it is.'

'Your luck's in,' she called over her shoulder, 'you

won't have to watch me ironing, I've already done it. And you're in for a good dinner, I thought I'd find only two eggs and some mouldy cheese in the fridge when I got back, but Gail's obviously been shopping.' There was enough food around to feed an army. She thought of Jack—Jack whoever he was. The man with the sense of humour. Maybe he had a voracious appetite, too. No sooner had she formed the thought than she realised . . . with Gail, anything might be happening.

'I've just had a horrid thought.' She went back into the living-room and looked worriedly at Gordon. 'Gail's coming home with some new bloke later but, well, knowing her she might have a party planned or something. All that food . . .' She didn't finish the thought. 'I'd better ring her in case I've been presumptuous.'

'What does that mean?'

'It means Gail might have had other plans for all the goodies I found. If that's the case, Gordon dear, I'm in for a telling off because I helped myself without thinking.' It was only as she picked up the phone that she realised the receiver wasn't nestling where it should be. It had been off the hook. She had plonked it down in the darkness earlier, and hadn't noticed. There was a high-pitched whining noise on the line and it was seconds before she could pick up the dialling tone. She dialled the number of the hospital and asked for women's surgical.

Gail answered on the first ring.

'Ah! That was a bit of luck. You're in your office—obviously!'

'Anthea! Thank goodness! I've been ringing and ringing you. You've been engaged for ages.'

'No, I left the phone off the hook by mistake. Sorry about that. I got in from Bromsgrove at——'

She was cut short. Gail sounded impatient. She must be busy. 'Never mind that. Now listen——'

'Sorry. Busy night, is it? Well, I just phoned to ask about all this food you've bought in. Steaks and whatnot. Did you have plans for it? Only I've got Gordon here and——'

'Anthea, will you please listen? Never mind the food! Eat whatever you like. I've had a phone call, it was over an hour ago, I've been trying to ring you ever since. I had to warn you because I'm not coming home tonight, after all. I'm spending the night with Jack, at his place.'

'Oh, Gail!' Anthea groaned. 'Isn't it a bit soon for that sort of thing? You've only just met him and——'

'*Don't* lecture me. Just *listen*.'

'All right, all right.' Anthea sat down, shrugging as she glanced over at Gordon. It simply didn't occur to her that the phone call Gail had referred to had been from someone other than Jack.

She was absolutely wrong about that. The telephone call had been from Aden and it had come via the international operator, who had a French accent. Aden, it seemed, was in Paris.

'Are you still there?'

Anthea couldn't speak. None of it was making any sense.

'He said he was in Paris, that he's tried to ring you at the flat and got no answer.'

'What—what did you say to that?'

'I told him what I thought of him,' Gail said firmly, 'then I slammed the phone down. Five minutes later he was on the line again and he bellowed at me so hard I thought he'd burst my eardrum. My God, that man's got a nerve! Who the hell does he think he is?' She gave Anthea no time to answer that one. 'Anyway, I thought

I'd better warn you.'

'Warn me?' Anthea's hands were trembling. It still didn't make sense, any of this, but it was enough to make her go pale. Not that she realised she'd lost her colour. Gordon saw it happening to her and he sat forward in his chair, signalling to her. She shook her head and held up her free hand. She could handle this. 'Gail, what do you *mean*? Warn me of what?'

There was a two second silence. 'Well, that he wants to talk to you, of course!'

'But——'

'Oh, Anthea, *I* don't know what he's up to, do I? He said he'd tried the flat several times over the past couple of days, and there had been no answer. He asked me where you were and I told him it was none of his business. He asked me again and I told him to go to hell, that there's no way you would want to talk to him. Did I do wrong?'

'No!' Anthea glanced desperately around the room, as if she were trapped. Stupidly she felt unsafe suddenly. It was seconds before she could bring logic into play. Aden was in Paris and she was in her home with Gordon. How safe could she get? She asserted herself. 'No, you did precisely the right thing. I don't want to talk to him and if he rings again, I won't. Gordon's here, he'll answer the phone for me. Thanks for the warning.'

'Right. I'll see you tomorrow, love.' There was a pause. 'What do you suppose he wanted?'

'Gail, I have no idea.' Which was accurate. But whatever it was, it was too much to ask. Anthea's equilibrium was delicate enough, she was getting through the days with difficulty as it was. If she heard Aden's voice, she would be in severe danger of breaking down.

When she put Gordon in the picture, he was furious. 'The bastard! He might at least have the good grace to leave you alone now.'

'He—has no idea how I feel about him, Gordon. He has no reason to think that contact from him would upset me.'

Gordon looked appalled. 'How can you defend him like that? The man's an out-and-out stinker. He's also stupid. My God, if you could only feel for me——' He stopped himself sharply. 'Sorry. Come on, let's eat.'

They both trooped in to the kitchen. The veg and the baked potatoes were ready, all that remained to be cooked were the steaks. Anthea put them under the red-hot grill and Gordon opened the bottle of wine he'd brought. The atmosphere had changed between them. It wasn't only because of the attempted contact from Aden, it was also because Gordon had let slip that he felt more for Anthea than friendship. They had both known it all along but while it had been unspoken, it had been all right, somehow. Now she was feeling guilty again. Much as she liked Gordon Langley, attractive though he was in so many ways, she felt not the slightest romantic interest in him.

Throughout dinner they talked shop, about various patients in the hospital. Gordon did most of the talking. It was only when Anthea made coffee a little later that an awful thought struck her.

Sybil!

That was it, it was the only explanation! She went pale again, and Gordon reached for her hand. 'What is it? What's——'

'Sybil!' She said the word as if it would explain everything, pushing herself to her feet as she spoke. 'I must find her last letter to me.'

'Anthea?'

She almost snapped at him. 'Sybil must be ill, don't you see? Aden's aunt, my friend——' Ill or—or something even worse. She dashed into her bedroom and rummaged in her drawer for Sybil's letter, her eyes scanning the top of the page. There was no telephone number on it. Of course there wasn't. At the time of writing it, they had not yet actually installed the telephone at the villa. She would have to ring International Directory Enquiries and keep her fingers crossed.

They came up with nothing. Firstly it was difficult to make herself understood. It wasn't that the operator was foreign, it was that she wasn't very bright.

'Well?' Gordon was as agitated as she by this time.

'Nothing. *Nada*,' she repeated in Spanish. 'They haven't got a record of the number yet—or so she said.'

'So what now?'

'There's nothing I can do. I'll just have to hope that Aden rings again . . .' Their eyes met. Hope that Aden rings? But she did. She was feeling frantic. And then she remembered the MacIntyres. 'The MacIntyres! I can ring them——' She reached for the telephone again and at the precise moment she did so, the buzzer went, the buzzer to the outer door downstairs.

'Bother!' Anthea did not put the phone down. 'Answer that, would you, please?'

Gordon did as he was asked while Anthea started dialling. A moment later, he was taking the receiver out of her hand. 'Don't bother,' he said. 'He's here. He's on his way up.'

Anthea stared at him. *'Here?'* But he was in Paris! 'Aden?'

Gordon looked at her solemnly. He nodded. 'Don't worry, I'll be right by your side.'

CHAPTER FOURTEEN

THERE wasn't time to say anything else. The doorbell rang and Anthea shot a look at Gordon as she moved to answer it. It was a mixture of panic and desperation. The instant she opened the door to Aden, she knew. Her worst fears were confirmed. She had never seen him looking so grave. Dressed in his dark blue overcoat, he stood gazing at her and there was pain in the green depths of his eyes. If Sybil were not dead, she was certainly very ill.

'Anthea——' Aden's eyes moved from her face, over her shoulder. Gordon was standing behind her. Aden's expression was one of disbelief. He looked from Gordon to Anthea and back again. 'What the hell are you doing here?'

'I might ask you the same thing.'

Anthea's hand tightened against the handle of the door. 'I—there's really no need for this. Come in, Aden.' She turned, trying her best to tell Gordon with her eyes that it was all right. She could cope. Well, she could, thanks to his presence.

The three of them moved into the living-room and stood, quite still, looking at one another. It was Aden who spoke first. 'I have to talk to you, Anthea.'

She nodded. 'It's Sybil, isn't it?'

'What?'

'Sybil. I—understand you've been trying to ring me.'

'I've been trying to ring you on and off for days!' He

almost spat the words. 'Where the devil have you been?'

'Now look,' Gordon stepped forward and faced him squarely. He was between him and Anthea now. 'Why don't you just say what you've got to say and get out of here?'

Aden glared at him with a look so venomous that Anthea thought there was going to be a fight. She reminded herself rapidly that both men were civilised human beings—whatever else they were or were not.

'Please!' She could hardly look at Aden, it hurt too much. Her eyes were fixed somewhere on his overcoat. 'Just tell me, Aden. Tell me what's happened to Sybil!'

'Nothing's happened to Sybil. To the best of my knowledge, she's absolutely fine. In fact she's never been more vigorous, believe me. Why should you think——'

'Then why are you here?' Gordon demanded. His face set, he moved closer to the dark man. 'What are you playing at, Aden? You can get out of here this minute!'

'Like hell. You're the one who's getting out. *Now!* What I have to say to Anthea is private——'

'Stop it!' Anthea felt sure she would be sick. The atmosphere was almost vibrating with anger, their anger. They stood, equally matched, both tall and broad and muscular, furious, glaring at one another. 'For heaven's sake!' Her voice rose, showing how panicky she was and telling clearly how near she was to tears. 'I—I want Gordon to stay. He—he came for the evening and——'

'So I can see.' Without turning, Aden jerked his head in the direction of the small dining table under the window. The debris of their dinner was still there, the empty wine glasses and the plates she had not yet cleared away. 'And very cosy it looks!' His eyes held accusation, accusation and . . . yes, pain! The pain was still in his eyes. Why *was* he here? If there were nothing wrong with Sybil, *why* was he here?

She turned at once to Gordon. 'Perhaps you'd better go. I——'

'I'm not leaving.' He moved, stood beside her and put an arm around her shoulders. Anthea took one look at Aden's face and knew without doubt that there was going to be serious trouble if she didn't make it plain to Gordon that she wanted him to go. 'No, I'm all right,' she told him. 'Please go, Gordon. If I need you, I'll ring you.'

The following few seconds seemed like hours. Gordon stubbornly said nothing, he stayed just as he was, protecting her, to his way of thinking. 'Gordon, please . . .!'

As Gordon turned to look at her, Aden's temper snapped. He took one long stride and grabbed hold of the blond man at the throat, his hand clenched around Gordon's collar and tie. 'Get out of here, Langley, before I throw you out bodily!'

Gordon moved like lightning. So did Anthea. The noise she emitted was approaching a scream. Before closing her eyes she saw Gordon knock Aden's hand aside and they both shifted position. They were going to murder one another, she was convinced of it. With eyes closed and her hands over her ears, she yelled at them at the top of her voice. '*Stop it!* Stop it, I tell you! If you have any consideration for me, *both of you*, you will stop this at once! I can't—I can't——' She couldn't finish her sentence, that's what she couldn't do. She had burst into tears.

She became aware of silence, stillness, she opened her eyes and found both men staring at her. Gordon muttered something to Aden which she did not catch, turned and spoke to her over his shoulder as he left the room. 'All right, I'll go.' He was back seconds later with his coat. 'I'm doing this for her,' he told Aden. 'Make no mistake about that. You don't frighten me, Aden. I'll leave you alone but I warn you, if you upset her or hurt her any more than you already have, I'll come looking for you and I'll take you apart limb from limb.'

He strode out of the room. Anthea chased after him feeling awful. She was trembling inwardly now, as well as outwardly. She felt sick to her stomach. 'Gordon—I—it'll be all right. Thank you, I——'

He put a hand to her cheek. 'I'm going to wait downstairs for a few minutes. If you don't open the door and call for me, I'll go home. But not before—I'll give you five minutes first.'

'All right.' She nodded, comforted, though she knew she would not call for him. Whatever Aden wanted, she was in no physical danger from him.

She walked back in to the living-room to find him standing by the mantelpiece, his back to her. 'A fine way for a doctor to talk,' he said.

'And coming from a barrister it's all right, is it?' Suddenly she was angry. It seemed to come from nowhere, it just welled up in her and burst forth. 'How dare you behave like that? Carrying on as if you were on the rugby field or something. If you really feel the need to tackle someone who's a damned good friend to me, you'll do it somewhere else!'

Aden ignored that. Very quietly, turning as he spoke, he asked, 'What did he mean, if I hurt you more than I already have?'

Anthea dropped her eyes. 'I've no idea.'

'And why did you refer to him as a friend just now?'

'Because that's what he is.' She was still looking at the carpet. 'A very good friend, very good indeed.'

'Very good indeed. I see.' He turned away again, and she looked at him. She could tell from the set of his shoulders he was fuming, trying to get control of himself. Not for the first time, she was at a loss to understand the man,

'You're doing it again, Aden, you're behaving as if I'm on trial! I'll thank you to remember——'

'I don't care what's between you two!' he cut in, spinning round to face her. 'I wanted to kill him, do you hear me? I still do!'

Anthea's breath caught in her throat. He was *jealous*. There were no two ways about it. 'Aden, I don't——'

'I'm in love with you,' he shouted. 'For God's sake, don't you know that? Are you blind? As blind now as you always were?' He moved towards her so quickly he was almost a blur. The next thing Anthea knew, his hands were on her shoulders and he was shaking her so hard that she thought her head would come loose. 'I don't care about him or anyone else! He's in your past as of now and I'm not *interested* in your past! I'm not interested in your boyfriends, your fiancé or your hang-ups. You're going to marry me, do you understand? *Do you understand me?*' He was shouting at her and somehow she found the ability to think in spite of his shaking her, just two thoughts. If he carried on like this, Gordon would start hammering at the door, Gordon and the neighbours as well. Aden was having some sort of breakdown, she thought simultaneously. She had to humour him!

'Yes, yes. Yes, I understand you. Now let *go* of me.'

He let go of her at once. He stood very still, looking down at her, and his apology was swift. 'I'm sorry,

Anthea. I'm sorry but I——'

She stepped away from him. She was safe now. All she
wanted to do was to get him out before she came apart a
the seams. 'Please leave, Aden. I can't imagine wh
you're here and why you're saying these things to m
but——'

'Anthea——'

'Stop it!' she yelled. 'For pity's sake, don't do this t
me.' It was she who was near hysteria now, with anger
with hurt and confusion. 'Don't *do* this to me! What d
you want of me? An admission that I'm in love with you
Is that it? I am in love with you. There is nothin
between Gordon and me. There never has been and ther
never will be because I love you, *you*. But I'll neve
forgive you for this, for coming here and doing this to m
Now get out, get back to your fiancée. Get out before
call the police and have you removed!

Anthea couldn't fight any more, she couldn't fight, s
she fled. She ran from the room and headed for th
bathroom. There was a lock on the door. She would sta
in there and come out only when he'd gone. She couldn
tolerate any more of this.

But she didn't even get as far as the door. Aden's arm
came around her, and immediately he touched her sh
collapsed against him, the tears coursing down her fac
'Aden, *please* . . .'

'Sssh.' He pulled her head against his chest, against th
roughness of the overcoat he still had on. 'It's all righ
that's what I'm here to explain. I'm not engaged to Fion:
Fiona is nothing more than a friend and colleague to m
You've got to believe that!'

'But——'

'The announcement in the paper was her ide;

She——' He broke off, as if realising his words couldn't be making sense to her. Very gently, he led her to the settee. 'Sit down, my darling. Don't cry any more, I can't stand it.'

And she couldn't help it. She had heard the words but they made no sense, she could feel her hand being held firmly by his, but she couldn't believe it was happening. She most certainly couldn't believe the things he'd said to her earlier. In love with her? Wanted to marry her?

Aden started talking then, unhurriedly but forcibly. He talked and she listened and it went on for a long time. As she listened, her emotions went full circle until she was almost laughing. Almost. She couldn't quite find it in herself to laugh. If the irony had not been so bitter, she might have succeeded.

'I've known Fiona for years. She is a friend, as well as a colleague, and I'm fond of her. But that's all. Until last November she had been living with her boyfriend, someone I know only vaguely and only through her. Fiona and I rarely socialise, we see each other mainly at work, which is enough, if you see what I mean.

'The man she was living with, for over a year, is a psychiatrist. She was introduced to him originally by David and Avis Freeman, the people whose party we were at on New Year's Eve. The two of them are friends of Fiona's parents. Are you with me so far?'

He smiled, looked at her questioningly but Anthea couldn't answer him except by nodding. She was intrigued to the point of silence and couldn't imagine where all this was leading.

'I'll assume that means yes.' Aden's smile broadened and he let go of her hand, he slipped his arm around her waist and held her closer instead. 'When Fiona moved in

with James Blackmore, the shrink, he was in the throes
of divorce. He asked her to marry him as soon as his
decree absolute was through. She's crazy about him. He's
crazy about her, too. Unfortunately, however . . .' he
paused, momentarily distracted. 'It's something I've seen
happen before, interestingly enough. When James's
divorce was finalised, he had second thoughts about
marrying Fiona. He stalled and he kept stalling for some
weeks. She flipped. It was my shoulder she cried on, it
was me she turned to for advice.

'I advised her to move out of his place. By the time I
actually said this to her, she had already decided to do
just that. She wanted to force his hand, shock him into
making his mind up one way or another. She knew that if
she continued living with him, he would start to take her
for granted and he might never get around to marrying
her. She wanted more than that, she wanted marriage. So
she moved out last November. By December she
discovered he was seeing someone else and she flipped
even further. Do you remember her phoning me that
night you and Sybil stayed at my house?'

Anthea nodded. She even managed to speak. '
remember it clearly.'

'Well, that was when she found out he was seeing
someone else. She wanted to come over to me straight
away and I would have let her, but the fog was too bad.
He sighed, shook his head and held Anthea even closer
'Since then I've been like an uncle to her. That is, until
she got it into her head that she could use me to make him
jealous. Or so she hoped. I went out with her a couple of
times before I left for Tenerife, purely so James would see
her out with me. I saw no harm in it. In fact I was quite

amused, I thought her the typically cunning female.' He paused, looking at her. 'What? No retort?'

'No retort.' It was then that she first started smiling. 'James was going to be at that party on New Year's Eve, wasn't he? No, he *was* there.'

'He was there, Aden confirmed. He looked grim. 'Fiona knew he would arrive sooner or later. He couldn't have avoided the party any more than she could. It would have taken too much explaining when the Freemans are good friends and it was a special occasion. Her parents were abroad for Christmas and the New Year—so she felt she had to go. Had her parents been able to, she might have avoided it.'

'Why bother? If she wanted James to see her with you, why avoid the party?'

'Because by then it was hurting her too much. Her little game had become painful. When she saw the girl James was taking out, which she did one evening when we were in a nightclub, she lost confidence. He was very attentive to the girl and while I didn't think she was particularly gorgeous, Fiona assured me she was. A model or something. I don't know.' He shrugged. 'Why I let myself get entangled like that, I can't imagine now.'

'You were trying to help a friend.'

Aden looked at her gratefully, seriously. 'Actually, yes. I was. Well, James duly turned up at the party on New Year's Eve and it was more than Fiona could handle.'

'He turned up with the same girl, the model?'

'Quite so. And Fiona——'

'Flipped even further.' Anthea was grinning now, not because she was particularly amused but because she had pre-empted Aden. 'Poor Fiona! And I thought ... thought she was jealous of your dancing with me.' She looked at him uncertainly.

He caught hold of her chin, planted a kiss on her nose. 'She hadn't the slightest interest in me. Romantically, I mean.'

She knew what he meant and she believed him. It was then that the irony of the situation, their respective situations, struck her. But she was still uncertain as she looked at him. 'Aden, I—there is nothing between me and Gordon, either. Can you ... I know how it looked, *appeared*, but do you believe me?'

He didn't seem sure. He looked deeply into her eyes, saying nothing. Then he kissed her, he kissed her for a long, long time, raising his head only when she had responded as she had always responded to him. When her eyes were wide and her pulses were pounding and her body was pressing closer to his. 'Aden——'

'I believe you.' His voice was almost inaudible. Anthea blinked, looking carefully at him. His eyes were suspiciously bright and—and then he was telling her again, almost croaking the words. 'I love you, Anthea. I love you so very much ...' He broke off, attempting a smile. 'I have to say it, I've been mad with jealousy. I believe you, my darling, but you've got to admit that the circumstantial evidence——'

When the telephone rang they both jumped violently. 'Who the hell——' Aden glanced at his watch. 'It's almost midnight! Who's ringing you at this hour?'

Anthea didn't dare say what she was thinking. It was Gordon, checking on her. It had to be. Lightly, she suggested she answer the phone and find out. 'Hello?'

'Anthea? Why do you sound so suspicious? What's up?'

She flopped back against the settee. 'Oh, Gail, it's you!'

'Are you drunk?'

'No. Yes!' She was drunk, drunk with happiness. She cuddled closer to Aden as she listened, wishing she could tell Gail everything. Some other time, she would do that some other time. For the moment she had only one thing to tell her. But she had to wait because Gail was doing the talking.

'. . . just going off duty. Jack's here . . . thought I'd ring and see if anything's happened. Have you heard from Aden?'

'Yes, I—actually he's here.'

'What?' Gail said it so loudly even Aden heard it. He grinned.

'Gail, will you calm down? You'll wake up half your patients!'

'What's going on?' she demanded. 'I thought he was in—I hope you're not alone with him? Is Gordon still there?'

'No,' Anthea said quietly. 'But don't worry, we don't need a chaperon, we're going to be married.' With that, she held the phone away from her ear. She was right to. Gail's demands for an explanation came in one long stream and on one breath. When she'd finished, Anthea put the phone back to her ear.

'All will be explained, my friend,' she said calmly. 'Tomorrow. Goodnight now.' She put the phone down and turned to Aden. 'She won't call back. She's intrigued to death but she has something better to occupy her mind right now. She has a new man. Now then, about this circumstantial evidence . . .' Anthea was business-like now. 'Mr Barrister, I wish to plead in mitigation.'

Aden looked at her. He got straight to the point. 'Gordon spent New Year's Eve with you. I mean he was here *all night*, Anthea. I followed you home from the party, I dropped Fiona off and came straight here, determined to talk to you. I parked at the back of the building and I saw Gordon's car there so I didn't come up. I watched your flat and I waited. Your lights didn't go off until five in the morning—and Gordon's car stayed right where it was. Fifty yards from where I was keeping vigil.'

'Spying, you mean!' She wanted to be annoyed but she simply couldn't. 'Aden Russell, how could you?'

'I couldn't not. So? I'm listening.'

'He walked home.'

'What?'

'Gordon. He walked home that night.' When Aden did nothing but stare at her, she went on. 'It's true. Obviously he left by the front door, so you wouldn't have seen him go. He walked because it's more than he dare do to drink and drive and I encouraged him to have a few drinks here because he'd abstained at the party, and after all, it was New Year's Eve. Apart from that, Gail was here, she was with me and Gordon every minute.' She went on to say more, much more, explaining how it was with her and Gordon, and why he was so good to her. 'He said he was doing it because someone was once good to him when he really needed a friend,' she finished. Then, shrugging, she added, 'But I do know he fancies me——'

Aden exploded at that. 'Fancies you? The man's in love with you! Have you no idea how lovable, how beautiful you are?'

She laughed, finally. She laughed gleefully. 'He is *not* that far gone. What bias!'

'Bias has nothing to do with this. I'm being perfectly objective now. I——'

'And you're playing for time,' she interrupted, laughing even more because it struck so many chords. He had accused her of playing for time in the past, when he had wanted to hear her say something she wasn't prepared to say.

'Now what are you talking about? You really are the most complex woman, you know.'

She nodded solemnly. 'Yes, darling. Now you'd better explain why you and Fiona announced your engagement in the newspaper. Wasn't that carrying things a bit far?'

'Too right it was. *She* did that. And she did *not* have my permission.' He looked so put out, so serious, that Anthea actually burst out laughing. 'It isn't funny,' she was informed. 'Can you imagine the shock I got when——'

'Can you imagine the shock *I* got?'

All the laughter faded. She was in his arms again, being held close, being stroked as though she were precious. 'Yes, I can. I'm sorry. Fiona asked me if she could put the notice in the paper. I said no, certainly not. I thought it—unethical is the nearest word I can think of. As you say, it was going too far. I had no idea she'd do it anyway, crafty little witch. She knew I was leaving for Singapore on the Thursday evening and she put the thing in the paper on the Friday, when I wouldn't be around to see it. Do you remember?'

Remember? Would she ever forget that day? 'I learned of it on the Saturday, when Sybil got Friday's *Telegraph*.'

'I know. What day is it today? I've lost track, what with the time differences and all.'

'It's Monday.'

'Monday? Well, I phoned the office from Singapore last Thursday, to tell them when I was coming back. I was informed that Sybil had been on the phone to them several times for the past few days, that she'd played hell when they said they didn't know how to reach me, which they didn't. Or rather they didn't know where to reach me because I hadn't bothered to let them know I'd moved out of my hotel and gone to stay in my client's house.

'Anyway, they gave me the phone number at the villa and I got on to Sybil straight away. That was when I learned what Fiona had been up to. At first I hadn't the faintest idea what Sybil was talking about. I hadn't seen any English paper. I was stunned. Equally bad—no, *worse*—my darling aunt wiped the floor with me. She demanded, she accused, she told me I was out of my tiny, convoluted mind. And I quote.'

Anthea was biting her cheeks now. 'Mm. I can imagine.'

'She said I must have gone entirely off my rocker because if *I* didn't realise I was in love with you, *she* did! Can you imagine it? There's no one quite like her, is there?'

'Not quite.' Laughter was bubbling up inside her again. She could guess the rest. 'And she told you I was in love with you, I'll bet.'

'She certainly did. She said you were heartbroken.'

'Heart——?' Anthea pulled away slightly, indignant. She had given nothing away to Sybil, she had taken the news extremely well. Or so she thought. A moment's reflection told her otherwise. 'My goodness, she's shrewd!'

Aden nodded. 'She should have been the lawyer in the family. She laid into me so hard I had to put her firmly in her place in the end. I told her to mind her own business, that I would sort it out. I shall look forward to talking to her in the morning. First thing in the morning. Anyhow, do you know what she had the cheek to say then?'

'Surprise me.'

'She said, "Sort it out? Sort it out! You're so mixed up, you'll be lucky to find your way back to England, dear boy." How do you like that?'

'Well, you're here.'

'Only just. It's a hell of a haul from Singapore and we had engine trouble at one point. We were grounded for hours. When we finally approached London, we had to divert to Paris because of the fog.'

Anthea put her hand to her mouth. No wonder he looked tired. And he had been here all this time without being offered so much as a drink or a cup of coffee. 'Oh, darling! I hadn't thought—hadn't realised you'd come all the way from Singapore. You must have come here straight from Heathrow?'

'Naturally. I thought I'd never get here. Luckily the fog lifted enough so we could come over from Paris.'

'I must make you a cup of tea at once.' But she didn't, not then. Aden merely laughed at her, took her in his arms and kissed her until she hardly knew what she was doing. She had to fight him off in the end. 'Aden! Let go of me now, there's something worrying me.'

'What?'

'I don't know, I can't remember!'

He smiled. 'Tea. You were concerned about my getting dehydrated.'

'No, it wasn't that. I mean—*Fiona*! Have you spoken to her?'

'I certainly have.'

Anthea groaned. Fiona had had the sharp side of Aden's tongue, she was in no doubt. 'You blasted her.'

'To put it mildly. I phoned her from Singapore. I also phoned you—umpteen times. Where have you been these past few days?'

'At home. I mean in Bromsgrove. With my parents. So what happened with Fiona? What did she say?'

'She said it had to be done, the announcement I mean, she said it was her last attempt at bringing James to his senses.'

'And did it?'

'As it happens, yes.' Aden smiled in spite of himself. 'James telephoned her instantly and played stink, demanded to see her at once. To keep it brief, they're going to be married at the end of the month.'

'Bravo.' Anthea was grinning. He didn't seem to appreciate that Fiona had in fact done him, and her, a favour. 'Don't you see?' she said, when she pointed this out to him.

'Of course I see.' He had hold of her again. 'In any case, my telling Fiona off had no effect at all. She was too happy to be perturbed by anything I could say.'

'That's love for you.'

Their eyes met and held. Suddenly there was no laughter, no words. For long moments they looked at each other and simply held hands. It was Aden who spoke first. 'I had never dreamt how much it can hurt.' When she merely nodded, he went on. 'That it can plunge one to the depths of despair or—or lift one to the heights of happiness.' He kissed the fingers of her left hand one by one, pausing at her ring finger. 'You will marry me, Anthea?'

'Just tell me when, my darling. Of course I'll marry you.'

'I . . . didn't know. Didn't know how you felt about me. I must be as stupid as Sybil says.'

'Then I must be just as stupid because I didn't know, either. I had no idea how you felt about me, you never said . . . you gave no sign.' But he had, in fact. She thought about that now, about his kindness, his tenderness when she had been ill in Tenerife. That had been her sign. But she had been so afraid, too afraid to see. Blind, as he had put it earlier. 'I—didn't want to love again.'

'I didn't want to love at all,' he admitted. 'You've no idea how much my thinking has changed, because of you. I should say thanks to you.'

No idea? Hadn't she? She smiled, and they talked on. They talked about the way their thinking, their needs, their wants, had changed. As had been the case in the past, they were of similar minds, very similar indeed. But what they both wanted for the future was so very different from what they both used to want. Or had thought they wanted.

'Going home at night,' Aden said at one point, 'it was—I couldn't believe how lonely I felt. It had never been like that before . . .'

A little later they were discussing, almost heatedly, how many children they would have. One, Anthea said. Two, Aden insisted. He was an only child and he didn't think it was a good thing. She capitulated, as she had known all along that she would. But she teased him for as long as she could, pitting her wits, her arguments, against him just for the fun of it. She informed him she would want to go on working, if only part-time, in private practice, perhaps. She told him they would have holidays together, plenty of them, and Aden dealt with it all. He said she could do that, that they would do all that, and that he didn't see what difference two children would make, given that he could afford as much help as they might need. 'Oh, all right! What's a child or two between friends?'

He reached for her and another half hour passed before he got his tea. It was very, very late by then. Anthea headed for the kitchen just as the telephone rang again. She gasped, knowing without doubt it would definitely be Gordon this time, and she turned around quickly to answer it. Aden picked it up before she could get there.

Anthea stood, both hands against her cheeks, looking anxiously at him as he spoke.

'Gordon!' he was saying, as if he were delighted. 'How lovely to hear from you, old boy! What? Of course I'm still here. My future wife and I were just going to have a cup of . . . yes, that's what I said. My future wife.'

Anthea retreated into the kitchen and stood by the sink, looking anxiously out into the night. After a moment or two, she dropped the Venetian blinds and put the kettle on. Aden's voice reached her from the living-room.

'Can you hear me, darling?'

'I can hear you. How—what did he say?' Poor Gordon, she was thinking. Poor dear! He must have been flabbergasted!

'Who? Gordon?'

'You know very well I mean Gordon! What did he *say*?'

There was laughter, mishchievous laughter. 'He said

e'll be there, that wild horses wouldn't keep him away.'

She stayed where she was, in the kitchen. 'Wild—what? Where? Where will he be?'

'At our wedding, of course,' came the casual reply. 'I might even ask him to be Best Man. Decent sort, Gordon Langley, I never did dislike him . . .'

Anthea retorted with something unladylike. Men! Would she ever understand them? When she emerged from the kitchen, tray in hand, Aden appeared to be asleep. She looked at his face, at every single detail of it, such a strong face, a handsome face. More importantly, such a dear, beloved face. 'Darling,' she said softly, loathe to wake him, 'tea's up.'

'Just resting my eyes,' he said, opening them. And then he was feasting his eyes. On her. 'I love you, Angel Face.'

'I love you, too,' she said quietly. 'More than words can say.'

Six exciting series for you every month... from Harlequin

Harlequin Romance·
The series that started it all

Tender, captivating and heartwarming...
love stories that sweep you off to faraway places
and delight you with the magic of love.

▼

Harlequin Presents·
Powerful contemporary love stories...as individual as the women who read them

The No. 1 romance series...
exciting love stories for you, the woman of today...
a rare blend of passion and dramatic realism.

▼

Harlequin Superromance®
It's more than romance...
it's Harlequin Superromance

A sophisticated, contemporary romance-fiction
series, providing you with a longer,
more involving read...a richer mix of complex plots,
realism and adventure.